A

Unknown

Love

Series

“The Damage of Deception”

Book 1“The Damage of Deception

Book 2 “Empty Vows”

Book 3 “An Unknown Love”

Book 4 “A promise broken”

Driving down this beautiful country road was breath taking to say the least.

With the trees lined up straight on both sides with their magnificent splendid of colors of gold, reds and orange, the sun peeking through the tree tops

This picture was nothing short of a masterpiece drawn out by the hand of God.

What peace and contentment on this beautiful fall day.

It wasn't that long ago I thought I had that peace and contentment, but as my memory soars back to six years ago it tells a different story.

Chapter one

I Knew I was running late and Coy would be upset with me

But it wasn't my fault, I had a dead line and I had just made it in time. Today Coy and I had an appointment to look at our dream house, we have worked hard, and save every penny we could to purchases this house, Coy was hoping we wouldn't have to go into debt. But this house was over our budget, but we both feel in love with it, I knew he was already there waiting for me, he had told me over and over "don't be late." I drove down the long drive that sold me on this house, it was beautiful... coy was standing on the sidewalk waiting for me, but I didn't see the realtor's car, so maybe she was also running late, and Coy wouldn't be too upset with me.

"Hey honey, sorry I'm late." "It's okay Lana is not here yet, she did call to say she was running late, I told her we would be in the back yard, he took my hand to lead the way

Do you really like it Sara?" Coy asked.

"Yes Coy I love it It's perfect, and not just because I'm so happy to be out of that tiny apartment" I said as we walked out to the back yard I could see the hopeful look on Coy's face, and I said a silence prayer that he wouldn't bring up the baby thing again, this was always a sore subject with me and he seemed to bring the subject up a lot lately, but before he had the opportunity to say anything the realtor walked up to us.

"Oh my goodness don't you just love this big back yard, so many possibilities here"

She said with a big smile

"Hi Lana, I would like for you to meet my wife Sara" Coy said.

"Oh it's so nice to meet you Sara" she extended her hand out to me.

She looked very professional in her dark green pantsuit, red lipstick and bleached blond hair with her sunglasses perched on top of her head.

It's nice to meet you Lana. I politely shook her hand.

As I listened to the two of them talk about the backyard, I wondered if there was going to be more to this house then this backyard...

"I would like to see the inside please" I said trying not to act to irritated.

"Oh of course I'm sorry" Lana said as she unlocked the back door.

"You are going to love this big kitchen do you like to cook Sara?'

"As a matter of fact I do not like to cook" I said with chuckle.

The kitchen was very big especially for a big family, next we went upstairs to the bedrooms, there were four of them, the master bedroom was very pretty, I loved it. with its big walk in closets, I could tell Coy was already sold on,

This house so after a quite tour of

The house we put our offer down.

Then I hurried back to my office promising Coy we would talk after I got back home.

Coy and I have been married for six years and I loved him with all of my heart, but we wanted different things in our future, Coy wanted children, a lot of them. He didn't come from a big family, and he had talked many times about the loneliness he had shared growing up, so that made him want a big family.

Every year I had managed to put him off on starting our family. But the truth was I never wanted children.

I thought after some time I would change my mind and actually want children, but I still didn't.

I have worked hard trying to get ahead in my career, a career I loved, I loved the big cites, the traveling, I love working for a million dollar company and to know that I'm successful at what I do.

I could understand that Coy wanted children, but why couldn't he understand that all I wanted to do was climb the ladder of success, and that I didn't have time for kids in my life right now or ever.

As I Walked in the door, I could see Coy was already busy at the table he had papers spread out all over it.

"What is all of this" I said.

"I wanted to wait until you got home to tell you in person, that Lana called and they accepted our offer."

"Wow that was fast"   I said. "I know I hope you are excited as I am"

"Oh Coy, I am. I can't believe after six year I'm going to have my very own walk in closet"

"And now we can start our family and I want to start right away" he said as he took me in his arms.

What a way to kill the excitement of a new home.

I thought.

"Trying to change the subject before it could turn to an argument, I said. " I can't believe I really get to move out of this tiny apartment?"

"Yes you do my love. Coy said.

Lana says it should take about a month and then we are out of here."

"Let's go out for supper to celebrate, I'll call Sandra and Scott.

I hopped up every step to our small upstairs bedroom to get dressed. I was so excited.

We met Sandra and Scott and the girls at the Restaurant;

Sandra and Scott were great parents.

Jaden was thirteen and Emma was eleven

And they were darlings, they loved their uncle Coy.

He was the happiest when he was around the kids.

"Okay we have news, I said, Coy and I just put an offer on our first house, and it was accepted so you are looking at future home owners."

"Oh Sara, I'm so happy for you guys, that is great."

"Thank you sis, it is great, I'm thrilled, and wait till you see it.

It is so big and beautiful, all hardwood floors"

"And the backyard is huge plenty of room for lots of children. Coy said all excited.

"How many bedrooms does it have Sandra asked

"Four bedrooms and three baths, and in the

master bedroom there is a humongous walk in closet."

"I think Sara likes the walk in closet the best about this house." Coy joked.

"I love everything about this house, but the walk in closet is a big bonus, and you should see the long driveway it has beautiful tree's that line both side of the drive.

It's very pretty. I can't wait to see it in the fall. Once we get moved in, we can have you guys over for a cook out, just like when we were growing up; remember Grandmother had big cooks out all the time."

"Yes I remember, especially when Uncle Scott would come and bring Scotty and I started to notice just what a cutie he was" Sandra laughed.

"Yea I remember how mean you two were to me, never letting me play with you guys, at those cookouts." I said as I gave them a mean look.

"Oh we're sorry but we were in love."

"You were six years old! I said.

After a nice visit and supper, we went home and it was all I do to keep from packing.

I wanted out of this apartment so badly.

"Coy let's go drive by the house again" "Honey its dark out, shouldn't we wait until tomorrow" "Yes of course you are right I guess I'm just impatient.

Chapter two

The next day at work, Sandra called to invite me to lunch.

We met at a little Café right down from my office, after we had eaten, Sandra looked at me and said, guess what?

"What?" I asked.

I'm pretty sure that I'm pregnant again"

"Oh Sandra I thought you were on the pill" "I want another baby, so a few months ago I stopped taking them." "Does Scott want another baby?"

"Scott wants a son"   "Sandra, you guys know there is a change it will be another girl Right?"

"We know, but we are willing to take that chance"

"How many kids do you and Scott plan on having?" "I don't know we haven't really discussed it, but I hope I'm pregnant and so does Scott."

"Well Then I'm happy for you." I said as I gave her a hug

"Thank you Sara, I can't wait until that day when you tell me you are pregnant"

"I wouldn't count on that Sandra"   "Why? You are going to be a great mother"

"No Sandra you are the great mother, I'm the great Aunt.

And that is how I want it to stay."

"You will come around just wait and see"

"Sandra, You know I have never wanted kids"

"But you have no idea what you are missing Sara, to hold that new born baby in your arms and to know it is your baby to keep and to take care of. It is so wonderful and I know you will love being a mom."

"No I won't love it. Because I do not want kids"

"So if something was to happen to Scott or myself you wouldn't raise my kids?"

"That is different" I gave her that I don't want to talk about it anymore look.

"Sara being a mom doesn't necessary mean you have to give birth to them, being a mom can also be someone that loves them and looks after them.

Just like a loving Aunt.

Chapter three

At last the closing day came for the house to be ours, Coy and I had everything all packed and we was ready to move,

Scott and Sandra came over to help

When everything was in the house it looked

As if we didn't have anything.

We took a break and the four of us went to eat, as we sat in a booth at the fast food diner, Sandra and Scott decided to confirm that they were indeed having another baby.

I could see the expression change on Coy's face and I hoped this wouldn't bring up the subject again about me having a baby. But all he said was

"Congratulation to both of you."

But I could tell it bothered him because he became quite, Sandra must have sensed it also "Hey so when are we going shopping for new furniture?"

"It will have to wait until I get back from Dallas at the end of next week "

I told her.

"Yes my traveling wife will be gone for a whole week" Coy said sarcastically.

I did not want to get into this same conversation every time I had to go away for my job, so I said nothing but now everyone felt uncomfortable.

"I guess it's time we get back to work guys" I tried to lighten the mood.

After Sandra and Scott left and we thanked them for all of their help.

I put a few more things away.

But it was getting late, and I was getting tired

"Should we wait until tomorrow to finish up?"

"Yea I'm ready to shower and get some sleep"

But after he showered and came to bed.

He went to sleep without kissing me goodnight, so I wondered if he was going to be upset with me during all of Sandra pregnancy.

Maybe he had married the wrong twin.

The next morning he seemed better, he was once again excited about our new home and was talking to me about all the plans he had for it, I was glad because I didn't want to leave tomorrow with him being upset with me.

I hated too leave for Dallas, I wanted to stay home and get my house fixed up, but I knew for now I had to dismiss my house and put all my thoughts into my job.

I did love my job and if we hadn't just moved in our new house, I would be very excited right now to be going to Dallas, for a whole week even though I did miss Coy when I went away for this long of a time.

And Coy hated it; we usually fought about me traveling so much.

If he had it his way I would be like my sister and be a homemaker and take care of his children.

Sandra, and I may be twins but we were the exact opposite from each other.

Chapter four

When I arrived at the airport, I rented a car and drove to the hotel

I had stayed at this beautiful hotel before and it was one of my favorites.

After dinning alone in the fancy restaurant, I went to my room to finish my layout for the next morning.

In the next few days I would meet with my colleague, this was one of the biggest deals we would make for our company and I had to be on top of it.

I called to talk to Coy before I went to bed; he was all excited and was going into details about what he wanted, concerning the house.

The next few days were very busy, but I felt confident that we had done a good job here in Dallas when we pitched our idea to them.

I came home two days early so now I could start on my new house without interruptions.

I could never tire of driving down this beautiful drive I felt so blessed to be able to call this place my home.

I was putting dishes away when Coy came home.

"Hey you have done a lot while I was away" I said as I gave him a hug and kiss.

"I have missed you Sara, I want to show you something" he took my hand and lead me upstairs. He was excited to tell me his plans.

"Okay I was thinking because this bedroom is next to the master bedroom I could put a door here so these two rooms could be connected and it could be the nursery what do you think?" "Coy I think when the time comes that will be a good idea, but I think we should hold off for just a little while.

Don't you think? I said.

"For how long this time Sara?" "Coy I just got home, we haven't seen each other for five days, and do we really want to have this conversation right now?"

"Okay, Sara you let me know when can we have this conversation?

Will it be when you are at your office, or hopping a plane to go thousands of miles away working for your awesome Job, as you call it?

"Coy, this awesome job is what paid for this expensive house that we wanted."

"Oh so just because you make more money than me, you get to call the shots in this marriage?"

"Coy that is not what I'm saying" I could feel the tears burning the back of my eyes.

"Than what are you saying? How long do you want to put me off now?"

"Coy be reasonable, we just moved in to this house can't we wait just a little while longer please."

He turned his face toward the hallway, and I could tell he needed that time to cool down. After a few seconds he turned to face me.

"Okay we can wait for one more year, but that is it Sara, after that no more putting it off."

"Thank you Coy, now can we please not be mad at each other, I hate it when we fight."

"Fine, he said, and then he gave me a hug.

But I could tell he was still upset with me.

On Saturday we went shopping for furniture.

We invited Scott and Sandra to go with us. I knew Sandra needed a break now and then from the girls.

We looked in a few different furniture stores, until I finally found furniture for the living room and the dining room also our bedroom.

By this time Coy was done looking and joined Scott in the Recliners to wait for us.

"The furniture will be delivered Monday afternoon Coy, so since you didn't want to help pick it out, you can't complain about it okay"

"I will like whatever you picked out, now can we go eat? I'm starved.

Chapter five

Monday morning when I walked in my office, there was a big cheer and the sound of a champagne bottle being opened.

"We got the deal?" I said as everyone that worked in the office cheered

"We got it. Thanks to all three of you. I give all you the highest praise and I want to say great Job!" my Boss looked very pleased today and I was glad, I felt proud of myself as I high fived my co-workers

I thought to myself, this is what my job is all about, I felt important and there no way I was stopping now.

Two months after moving into our new house it was completely furniture. And it was home,

We were having our first cook out with the family before the weather turned cold.

"You have a beautiful home here Sara" "Thank you Debra, I'm so glad you could come today"

I had always had the feeling that Debra did not like me, I didn't know why, Debra was his only sibling. Both their parents had passed before I had met Coy.

Coy spend a lot time with Jaden and Emma playing cards games with them,

I didn't understand why this wasn't enough for him, just to be around Sandra and Scott's kids, why did we have to have them, to me it was so much better , because I didn't have to be responsible for them and when I had to away on a business trip. I could just go,

I liked my life the way it was, I just wish my husband did.

I was always happy around Christmas time and I was looking forward to celebrating it in my new house

Coy helped me decorate for the holidays , we had invited the family over for a Christmas eve party, Coy dressed up like Santa and the girls loved it, almost as much as Coy did. I told him the girls were too old for Santa, but it didn't matter, and I liked it that they humored their uncle.

Sandra said we spend way too much money on the girls, but I thought to myself, better yours than mine.

Sandra was starting to show a lot, I could tell Scott was so happy because they had found out they were having a boy.

"So since you guys are having a boy, will this be your last one?" I asked

"We haven't discussed that yet"

I felt like I needed to stay off of that subject with my sister.

"So have you two picked out a name yet?" My Dad asked.

"Yes we have, we are naming him after Scott's dad and after you dad" Sandra proudly said.

"Luke Scott Allen" "I like that" I told her.

I really wanted to change the subject about babies.

So I jumped in with the news I had.

"So Coy has a few days off for the holidays, so he is going with me to Los Angeles.

It gets pretty lonely there, site seeing by all by myself."

"Oh wow you two will be able to get out of the cold for a while I envy you" Sandra said.

"I wish you guys could go, we could have so much fun."

"Maybe one day but now anytime soon." She said as she put her hands on her stomach. "Well maybe one day" I said.

Chapter six

I Was excited I would get to wear my sandals In January, I loved packing my summer clothes when it was snowing outside.

The weather was perfect, we took long walk on the beach, and I felt like I was on my second honeymoon.

I wasn't ready to come back home, I was having a good time with Coy, and enjoying the beautiful weather.

The winter seemed to drag by, and it was nice to see spring arrive.

Scott called me on my way to work, to let me know Sandra was in labor.

"Oh that's great; call me when he is born." "You won't be coming to the hospital?"

"Of course I will come by on my way home from work"

"Okay I will tell her that." Scott sounded disappointed?"

I called Coy to let him know I was going to the hospital after work.

When I arrived at the hospital, Sandra was holding the baby he was so tiny and all red

"Hey Sis how are you doing?" "I'm great, just look at him isn't he beautiful?"

"Wow I sure didn't see what this momma saw. To me he was far from beautiful.

"Okay mommy, we need to take this little guy down and get him weighted" the nurse said as she took the baby from Sandra.

"So did you have an easy time with him?

" I asked.

"I think he was easier than the girls,"

Coy knocked on the door. "Hey can I come in?"

"Yes coy, you can come in" Sandra said

"Well congratulations again on your new son." Coy told her.

"Thank you, have you seen him yet?"

"No I haven't, Sara would you like to go with me?"

"Sure, Sis we will be right back"

Why did I dread to go to the nursey and see this baby with Coy? I was getting so tired of having to watch every word I said as to not bring up the baby subject, this had to stop I have to tell Coy the truth that I'm never going to have a baby.

I knew in a few months my year will be up, and he is going to expect me to give him a child.

Scott and Aunt Tina were standing at the window watching as they weighted him and did all the measurements they do to newborns.

"Do they keep the babies in a nursey here?" I asked Scott. "No they will take the baby back to Sandra soon"

"You are a lucky man Scott" "Thanks Coy I know I am."

"So when are you two going to have a baby?" Aunt Tina asked.

"We are going to start soon" Coy told her. I didn't say anything, I just smiled

And told Coy, I would see him at home.

Aunt Tina and I walked back to Sandra room to tell her goodbye.

"You have a very handsome boy" Aunt Tina told her.

"Thank you Aunt Tina"

"Okay Sis, I'm going home now, if you need anything let me know"

"Okay I will, thanks for coming"

"I have to go also, Paul has the girls at the church, we are taking them out to eat, and I'm sure they are waiting for me.

Coy came home a little while after I got home.

"I will have supper ready soon "

When we had finish eaten, Coy ask if we could talk.

"Sure what's up?" "Sara I want to start our family now, I just can't wait any longer besides a

few months is not going to make that much difference"

"Coy I agree we do need to talk, but please just hear me out, and try to have an open mind please."

"Oh no Sara you are not going to tell me you want to wait until next year because I'm sick of you putting off having a baby, we have been married seven years and I have waited without complaining but not anymore,"

"Coy I know how much you want children and I understand that, but why is it too hard for you to understand that I don't want children."

"What do you mean you don't want children? How long do you want to wait?"

I could tell he was losing his temper with me he stood to his feet.

"Coy sat down and let me tell you something please."

He sat down and I could see this conversation wasn't going to be like the one I had planned out in my head.

"Coy with my job and all the traveling I do and even you on the occasions when you go with me we have fun, don't we?

Right now we are in the position to do what we want, if we want to leave and go somewhere we can.

We can travel and see places and do things we could never see if we had kids.

Coy, you know I love my Job so I can't understand why you would want to ruin all of that by having kids, why do we have to change or lives? Can't you be contending the way things are?"

"So how long are you saying you want to wait before we have kids?" he said as if he didn't just hear a word I said.

You didn't understand anything I had just said, did you?"

"How long?" he sounded very demanding.

"Coy, I don't want children now or ever I'm sorry but it doesn't take children to make us happy, haven't you been happy? I know I have been. I'm very happy just being with you, isn't that enough?" I pleated.

Coy just looked at me for a long time without saying a word then he walked out the door.

I couldn't believe he would just walk out like a spoiled child that didn't get his way, why should I want a baby I already had one.

I just sat there for the longest time then I got up and cleaned the kitchen, when he still hadn't returned I started getting a little worried.

It had been hours and he still wasn't home.

I feel asleep on the couch, I heard him come in and go into the bedroom

I stayed on the couch, waiting for him to apologize, but he didn't.

I didn't get a lot of sleep, I hoped he thought about what I said last night and would come to realize I am right, and hopefully we can put this all behind us and move on.

Chapter seven

The next day Sandra came home from the hospital so I stopped at her house after work

The girls were so happy to have a baby brother.

"Sandra do you need me to do anything while I'm here?" "No I think we are fine, but thank you"

"I held baby Luke for a while then I went home to face whatever mood Coy would be in.

I was shocked to see he picked up pizza for supper, and glad I didn't have to cook

He didn't seem mad, he just seemed distant.

So for the next two weeks, he would eat supper, watch TV, and then go to bed.

If I would ask him a question, he would answer it, but he didn't talk to me. But tonight I had enough.

"Coy we have to talk about this, we can't go on not speaking, and you are acting like a child."

"Sara I'm not going to fight with you" "I'm not asking you to fight with me, I'm asking you to talk to me" I snapped at him.

"Well I don't want to talk to you" "Coy, you act like you want me to leave?'

"Would you please" he said.

My heart was crushed I was expecting him to say No, I don't want you to leave but that is not the answer I got from him.

And it made me mad.

"No I will not! you leave Coy; if you can't talk or be civil to me" then just go."

I ran up the stairs to our room before he could see me cry, a few minutes later I heard him leave, two hours passed and he still hadn't returned.

And then Sandra came over and I was really surprised to see her because she hardly ever left her house especially without a toll of kids.

"Hi Sis, come in" I opened the door wide for her to enter.

"Sara, Coy is at my house and he is really upset."

"So instead of talking to me he runs to you! This is just great" Now I was getting annoyed.

"Sara, he told Scott and me what you told him.

And quite frankly I can't believe it, you know how much Coy has wanted children, and he has waited for you very patiently, while you get your career where you wanted it.

"Exactly and now that I have my career where I want it, I'm supposed to just throw it all away to give Coy a child?" I am where I want to be and I can't understand why you or Coy can't understand that."

"But Sara, you can still have a career and children." have you even took his feelings into consideration, is your marriage all based on what you want?"

"No of course not but I can't have a baby just to please my husband."

I don't expect you to understand Sandra, but growing up it was you who always talked about being a mommy.

You and everyone in our family knew I never wanted that, while you were dressing up in flats pretending you were going shopping with your kids, I was dressing in heels and carry a pretend briefcase to my office."

"I remember Sara, but we are not kids anymore and now you have a real husband to deal with, and consider what he wants."

"I know and in time Coy will come around and see that I'm right..."

"I hope you are right sis."

"Sara, having children shouldn't be that big of a deal, you should want to give your husband children."

"Really Like you Sandra, let's see Jaden is thirteen Emma is eleven, and now Luke

Is this your career Sandra having babies? Cause that is sure not mines."

You can't understand why I don't have children and I can't understand why you don't stop having them, don't you feel like you are taking away from your kids by having more and more.

I knew I was just mad at Coy, and I was taking it out on her, because I felt like she should be on my side not his.

"Don't get me wrong I love my nieces and nephew.

But it's not for me, Sandra you know I have never wanted children, and I thought you didn't either that's why you gave Jaden up at her birth"

I knew I had gone too far when I saw the hurt look on her face.

"Sandra I'm sorry I didn't mean that. I know how much you love your children and I know how much you have sacrificed for them, but please understand it's not for me, and I need you to stop judging me for not wanting kids."

"It's not that I'm judging you Sara, I just don't want to see two people that love each other to just throw that away."

"I know, but Coy and I will work it out."

After Sandra left, I laid on the couch and fell asleep waiting for Coy to return it must have been very late when I heard his key unlocking the door.

I sat up on the couch.

"Coy can we talk?" "Nope I have nothing to say, good night" and he started toward our bedroom.

"Coy we have always talked about what is bothering us" I cried. "Really well this time Sara, I don't think we can."

"Yes we can Coy talk to me, tell me how you feel."

"Tell you how I feel? Does it matter? I thought the only feelings in this marriage were yours!"

"Coy that is not true and you know it" with a mean look on his face he began.

"Okay you want to know how I feel? I will tell you, I feel like for six years you have lied to me, I believe you have never intended on having children with me, and every month for the last six year my heart would break a little every time I found out you wasn't pregnant.

And right now I'm hurt and to be honest with you I can't stand to be around you right now!"

He went upstairs, and I heard him close the bedroom door.

I couldn't believe he just spoke to me in that manner with those very hurtful words.

I stayed on the couch but sleep didn't come, but tears did.

At five in the morning I got up and showered, got dressed and went to the office

I couldn't keep my mind on my work, because Coy's words kept playing over and over in my head.

Chapter eight

I had to go to Denver the next week for a presentation, but with my circumstance and the fact that my husband just told me he didn't want to be around me I decided to go talk to my boss about going a week early, I needed time to figure things out.

When I went home to pack my bag, I was glad Coy wasn't there, so I hurriedly packed my bag and drove to the airport.

I was so tired I napped on the plane something I never do.

After I checked into my room, I walked to a little park across the street from the hotel.

Everything was so beautiful here with the tall mountains I sat on a bench and took in all the scenery, I wish I could just stay here forever and forget about my problems, but I couldn't. I already missed Coy so badly.

How I wish he was here sitting beside me. I watched as couples walked passed me, holding hands, and my heart hurt.

After a while I got up and walked down to a café to eat dinner,

I still couldn't eat I didn't realize just how Cody's words had hurt me.

Those words were the only thing that kept me from picking up the phone and calling him.

I was wondering if maybe our marriage wasn't as strong as I thought it was.

After eating what little I could and keeping it down, I walked down town to look in the little antique shops.

I started getting tired so I went back to the hotel, took a shower, and went to bed; I was exhausted from the night before.

I spend the whole week walking, taking in all the beautiful scenery, I spend a lot of the time sitting on a bench in the park, I felt good there, it made me feel relaxed.

I tried to keep my mind off of Coy, because I knew in my heart I could fix everything, by giving him children, but I also knew it would only fix it for a while then how long before I was start resenting him.

Somehow I got through my presentation, but I knew I could have done a better job if my Mind hadn't been so distracted, I was just glad to be heading home, maybe Coy had calmed down and he will be reasonable and talk to me.

The plane ride home was not happy but more of a dread I didn't want to have another confrontation again with Coy, it didn't matter what condition my marriage was in, I still couldn't even consider having a baby even if it meant saving my marriage.

When I got home the only sign of Coy was a letter he left for me on our dresser

That read......

"Sara I'm sorry but I'm having a worst time of this than anyone could imagine.

I just need some time away to try to figure out things, Sara I want a baby, a family more than anything and now I know I can never have that with you." It was just signed... Coy.

It was at that moment I knew just how much I loved Coy because my heart was being ripped out of my chest, I called his cell, but it went straight to his voice mail. Coy please call me we can work this out, I love you. I know if we just sat down and talked about it, we can come up with something that will be fair to both of us please call me.

Chapter nine

IT has been three weeks and I still hadn't heard from Coy, I have left Message after message on his voice mail.

I couldn't keep my mind on my job I couldn't sleep I was making myself sick.

One day my boss called me into his office.

"Sara is there something going on with you; I know you told me, you and Coy were having

problems. And that is why you wanted to go to Denver a week early.

But Sara, I have an office to run here, and when you slack off on your work, and I have people waiting for our proposal, they are not going to wait for your broken heart to heal, they are going to move on."

"I'm sorry, you are right, I promise to get it together."

I need that presentations on my desk by the end of the week, or I will have no other choice but to give the assignment to someone else.

I do sympathize with everything you are going through and I'm here if you ever want to talk, but like I said we have a job to do here."

"I know you are right and at the end of the week it will be on your desk, I promise.

After work I didn't go home, I went to Sandra's house.

"Hi Aunt Sara" Jaden and Emma ran up to me "Aunt Sara I have missed you so much" they said in unison "Oh I have missed you guys too so much.

"Where's Luke?" "I just got him down, he is not feeling good"

"I hope it's nothing serious" "no I'm pretty sure he just has a tummy ache, because he has been cranky all day."

"Sandra, can we talk?" "Certainly

Girls go to your rooms so your aunt and I can talk please"

"Sandra, Coy left three weeks ago and I can't get a hold of him, he won't return my calls have you heard from him?"

"No I haven't Sara I'm sorry."

"None of this makes any sense, I mean did he even love me, because I don't know how you can love someone and then just leave them" as much as I tried not to cry, I just couldn't hold back the tears.

"Sara I know you love Coy, just like I know he loves you.

So with that being said couldn't you reconsider giving him a baby? For the sake of your marriage"

"Oh my goodness I'm sick of having this same conversation over and over.

"Don't get upset Sara I'm trying to help you, I don't want to see your marriage fall apart,"

"Sandra, I'm not upset, I'm tired and I'm hurt to think he would leave me, leave our marriage just because I don't want kids"

"I'm sure once Coy gets over this he will come back Sara, tried not to worry, Coy loves you."

We both know that" She sounded confident.

"Well I used to think that, but now I'm not so sure, Please tell the kids goodbye for me."

"Sis I'm here if you need me, if you just want to talk, I will come to you okay."

"Okay thanks." I gave her a hug goodbye.

The next day when I was at work Coy called me to ask me to meet him for lunch.

I thought At last now we can talk.

He was already at the café when I arrived he looked as bad as I felt.

"Hi Coy how are you?" Fine have a seat this won't take long" he said matter-of-factly

"Sara I have given this a lot of thought,

And I have decided that I want a Divorce.

"Coy you can't be serious I thought you loved me?"

"Sara it has nothing to do with love, we both want two different things in life.

You want your career And I want a family and let's face it.

It won't work with us anymore. So it is best that we end it now and go on with our lives."

"But coy, you are my life." I was so mad at myself for crying in front of him.

"Don't you think what we had this last six years has been good, I love you, and I thought you loved me?

"I thought I did too, but right now I'm not sure anymore, and I'm thinking a divorce would be best for both of us, that way we can both move on."

He got up to leave and I felt like a fool sitting there alone crying, I could tell people were looking at me, I quickly dried my tears and left.

Now I was just mad, I called my office to tell them I was taking the rest of the day off and I drove to Coy's work.

When I pulled up at his office he was standing outside talking to some men he had a clipboard in his hand writing things down.

I marched right up to him; I didn't care at this point who heard what I had to say.

I have talked in from of many important men before, it didn't bother me.

"Coy I need to talk to you right now." I demanded.

"Sara, this is not the time, nor the place"

Totally ignoring his statement...

"So you are telling me if I don't give you a baby, you are going to divorce me? Is that it?

"Sara this is not the place to have this conversation please go"

"No I will not go! Not until you talk to me" he roughly grabbed my arm and led me where no one could hear us.

"Sara It's over! Go back to your fancy office maybe if you're lucky you can go on one of your fancy trips but just go away"

"Coy please don't do this, I will have a baby for you if that is what it takes.

"Go away Sara"

He walked back into his shop.

There was nothing more that I could do, in my wildest dreams I never thought or even considered that by me telling him I was never having children would end my marriage but now I know Coy never loved me.

Chapter ten

He was not going to win this, this is crazy, how could he divorce me for not wanting children, this is insane.

I went back to my apartment and spend the rest of the day in bed crying.

I knew the next day I had to get my work done, I had promised my boss and I didn't want to let him down.

The house I used to love was now just big and lonely without Coy, I hated staying here alone.

Three months have passed since Coy left me and filed for a divorce.

And every day it didn't get easier like everyone told me it would.

But it gets harder with each passing day.

Michael and his girlfriend came over every day trying to get me to go out with them.

Michael hated Coy for what he was doing, and he couldn't understand why I still loved Coy, but I did.

I made Michael and Sandra promise me they would not tell dad, I really thought by now Coy and I would have been back together.

I knew I couldn't live here anymore and take the chance of running into Coy with another woman, I had to get out of here, everywhere I turned there was something that reminded me of him.

I was sick every day my nerves were shot, I needed a change, apparently my marriage was over so why should I stay here just to get hurt all over again and again.

I thought we had the perfect life, we have this beautiful home, and we have our jobs and family, why did he want to change that.

Somehow I had to talk to Coy, before I made my decision to leave.

I left one more message on his cell phone

"Coy if you won't give me ten minutes of your time I will be at your work every day starting today , I need for you to call me and tell me that our marriage is over and you are going through with this divorce, because if you tell me yes, then I'm leaving here and I'm leaving this house. I will not allow you to keep hurting me over and over."

Five minutes later he called, but I found out very fast, I was not ready for the truth.

"Sara, I'm going through with the divorce, and I'm willing to pay you back haft of the money we have invested in the house, but to answer your question. Yes this marriage is over, goodbye.

He didn't give me a chance to speak. I decided right then and there I was done crying and now I'm taking charge and protecting my heart.

The next morning as soon as I got to work, I told my boss the entire story, he sounded very sympathetic.

I asked him about what he thought of transferring me to Denver.

He said he would check into it for me.

A few days later my Boss told me that if I was sure that they would love to have me in Denver.

"Sara we will miss you here and if for any reason it doesn't work out there. Your job will always be open here"

"Thank you so much, working here has been a great experience for me and I have loved my job here, I do appreciate everything you have done for me.

I wanted to tell Sandra first, so I called her from my office.

"Hey Sis can you leave the kids and Scott tonight and have dinner with me.

I need to talk"

"I would love that, I haven't been out of the house in a while, let me call Scott at work and I will call you right back."

I met her at the restaurant after work, she seemed so happy to see me or just to be out of the house away from kids for a while. I wasn't sure which.

"Sara, honey you look terrible. Are you eating, or getting any rest?"

"Well I'm sleeping now pretty good, but eating is another story because of my nerves and everything that has happened, I get sick a lot"

"Sara, you can't let this make you sick." "Hey I didn't ask you here so you could tell me how bad I look" I laughed.

"Okay sorry."

"Sandra I'm moving to Denver at the end of the week"

"What, are you serious?" Her voice got a little loud, and a few people turned to look at us.

"Yes I'm transferring there, and all the paperwork is being done now, my boss said I should be able to leave at the end of the week"

"Oh Sara, that is such a long ways away."

"I know it is a long ways but please try to understand if I stay here, I'm going to run into Coy, it's bound to happen and I can't stand the thought of seeing him with someone else."

"I do understand, I just hate it that you are leaving,"

"Sandra, I need a new start somewhere else and I love Denver, and you can come out to visit me"

"Get real. I never get to go anywhere, but grocery shopping, I'm sorry I didn't mean that the way it sounded, I love my kids and my life with Scott."

"I know you do, you are a good mom, but even good moms need a break sometimes."

After promising her, I wouldn't leave before I came to see her, I went to my Dad's.

I wanted to get this over with and mark it off my list, so I decided to tell all of them.

I hated to tell him, because I knew he was going to try and talk me out of moving.

I also had to tell him about Coy and I, my Dad was very fond of Coy; it was him that had arranged our first date.

"Hey sweetie, what a pleasant surprise come in"

"Hi Dad, after hearing about everything that was going on with them and then Michael,

I had a feeling I was going to be here for a while.

"Dad I need to tell you something, it's not going to easy, so I'm just going to come out and tell you."

"Well that has always been the best way for me, what is it Sara?'

"Coy and I are getting a divorce" "Why? I thought you guys had the perfect marriage; you just got that beautiful house

I thought so to, but our problem is kids, Coy wants them and I don't"

"And you feel like that is a reason to end your marriage?"

"No I don't, but unfortunately Coy does." "I don't understand you have always known that Coy wanted kids, so what? You just changed your mind and decided not to give him any?

"Dad you know I have never wanted kids, and yes I have been putting off having kids and I thought maybe one day I would want one, but I don't want kids ever and that's the bottom line."

"Don't you feel like this is something you should have talked about before you got married? Sara, you need to be reasonable and think about this before you let this pull your marriage apart."

"Dad my marriage has already been torn apart and I can't fix it, so that is why I came here to tell you I'm moving to Denver."

"Denver? So you are just going to run away from all of this and just give up?"

"Please understand I have no choice, if I stay here I will see Coy with someone else and I just can't handle that." And then the tears came.

"Oh honey don't cry, this can be worked out" My dad took me into his arms and he didn't say anymore until I had stopped crying.

But when I had dried my tears he started again.

"Sara please is reasonable. You are moving to Colorado where you don't know anyone."

"Dad maybe that is what I need and besides I have my job."

"But honey your family is here"

"Mike leave her alone she is a grown woman with a good head on her shoulders she will be fine" Tami came to my rescue.

"Dad I will only be a few hours by plane please try to understand, I need to start somewhere else new."

"You know I will support you on your decision, I just hate to see you leave."

"I know Dad, but I will be fine."

After I left there I decided to wait until the next day to tell grandfather and Aunt Tina.

I went home feeling kind of depressed, was I making the right decision by going to Denver.

Chapter eleven

When I awoke the next morning after a good night's rest I felt a lot better, even a little excited about my move.

After work I went to my grandfather's to tell him and to visit with him.

He was starting to look old, not getting around as he used to, he talked about retiring from the church, he was supportive of my decision to move to Denver, but he was very sad about our divorce.

After I left him, I went to my Aunt Tina's house to tell her goodbye.

"Sara, hi come in it's been a long time, I miss you girls.

"Aunt Tina, I'm not sure if maybe you have heard or not, but Coy and I are getting a divorce"

"No I haven't heard that. Oh my goodness I'm so sorry, Sara there has to be a way, you two seemed so happy, what changed that?"

"Coy wants children and I don't. And when I told him this, he left me and we have talked and it's not me that wants to end our marriage, I love my husband very much, but apparently he didn't love me enough to stay."

Aunt Tina gave me a hug, sweetie, I know the hurt of a failed marriage, and I'm so sorry

Paul and I will be praying for you"

"Thank you Aunt Tina, also I come to tell you goodbye, because in a few days I will be moving to Denver, my job is sending me there."

"Oh no, can't you tell you don't want to go, you don't know anyone in Denver, you will be all alone without your family."

"It was at my request that I move to Denver, I need a fresh start."

"I can understand that, I will miss you, but you will come back to visit right.

"Yes after some time has passed and I have gotten over Coy.

After a short visit I told her goodbye.

"I love you Sara" "I love you Aunt Tina.

"You call me, if you ever need anything or you just want to talk okay."

"Okay I promise."

On my way back to my home Michael called me on my cell.

"Hey Sis, First of all, I will miss you and I wish you would change your mind about leaving, but I know your mind is made up to go, and I can't say I blame you, everyone needs a new start sometimes."

"Thank you Michael."

I think it's time for me to make a fresh start also and move out of my parent's home."

So I just wanted to let you know I'm proud of you sis."

"I will miss you, but you can come to Denver to visit me." "I will, Love you sis."

It broke my heart to pack my things and put them in my car, I loved this house and I kept thinking about the day we moved in, we were so very happy, or I should say I was very happy.

How did all of this change? I wanted my life back I wanted my husband back.

With a loaded car and a broken heart, I was on my way to a brand new start in life.

And I was scared, scared of the unknown.

After four hours of driving, I was parked on the side of the road throwing my guts up.

This was not going to be a fun trip, I had never traveled very far by car, and my body wasn't used to it, beside my nerves were a wreck.

After eight hours of driving I got a room for the night

The next day my experience was about the same.

I thought about Coy and my family as I drove how much I missed them and how much I missed my life with Coy.

It's funny how fast your life can change, one day we are picking out furniture for our home, and now I'm here in my car traveling hundreds of miles away from everyone, for the first time in my life I am truly alone and I cried.

I was so glad to see signs to Denver it was going to take a month for me to recover from this long trip.

I drove around for a while looking for the B&B I had rented for a week hopefully it wouldn't take longer than that to find me a place to live.

After I met and talked to my new land lady, I unpacked my car, than I laid down for a nap.

I slept the whole night, I must have really been tired, but I felt refreshed, and ready to start my day.

After a quick shower, I drove downtown to have something to eat and to check everything out

The cold air felt good .Hopefully I wouldn't throw up again.

I still couldn't eat a lot for fear of being sick again and nothing taste good to me anymore.

After some site seeing, I went back to my room.

I was already the next morning to start my new job even though I had been to this same office many times it had never been my home office until now.

Everyone was especially nice to me and welcomed me.

There was an older lady there, she was about to retire, she took me under her wing.

And mothered me a lot, I lost my mother at a very young age, and being away from my family, she was just what I needed at this time in my life.

When Jan, found out I was staying at the B&B downtown, she went out of way to help me look for my own place, when after a week we still hadn't found anything, she insisted on me staying with her until I found a place.

"Jan, no I can't put you out, I will be fine and I'm sure I will find something soon".

"Dear, you will not be putting me out, I live alone in that big old house, and I would love it if you stayed at my home.

Chapter twelve

By the end of the week, I moved what little things I did have into Jan's house.

I didn't have a lot because I left everything in the house. I didn't want to bring anything that reminded me of Coy.

Jan was constantly fussing over me, making me delicious meals, and the smell from the cooking made me so sick, but I couldn't let her know that.

It felt so good to have someone that cared about me in Denver.

One Morning I was in the bathroom throwing up, when Jan knocked on the door.

"Sara, are you okay?' " Yes I will be right out" I answered her.

"Sara, this is the second time I have heard you throwing up, how long has this been going on?"

"For a while now, I thought it was just because of the Divorce, and my nerves, but now I don't think so.

Jan, I think I might be pregnant." I cried

She held me while I cried. "I'm going to make you a doctor's appointment at my doctor's office they have an obstetrician there. "Thank you Jan"

Four days later the doctor only confirmed what I already knew, but when The Doctor said the words, it make it real, I was having a baby.

"Sara, you are almost five months pregnant, and you didn't know?" the doctor looked at me strange.

"I thought it was because of everything I was going thought until recently I started suspecting that maybe I was."

"Didn't you feel movement?" She asked.

“Yes but I didn’t know or maybe I have been in denial, She made me feel like an idiot.

“I’m sorry but I just feel like this is an unwanted pregnancy.”

“Yes it is, but that’s beside the point.”

“I want to do an ultrasound in a next week, I’m starting your blood work today and your prenatal vitamins.” The Doctor was saying.

“Okay, thank you Doctor Olson”

On my way back to the office, I had a thousand thoughts running through my mind. Coy was getting the baby he wanted, we can fix our marriage now, I can move back home where all of my family was, but most of all I will be with Coy.

I hated to leave Jan, but I knew she would understand.

I talked to my new boss and I told her the whole story.

"Sara I understand you predicament, but will you take some advice from an old woman?"

"Certainly, but you are not an old woman."

"Well okay an older woman than yourself, how's that's?"

"Better" I said with a smile.

"I'm going to give you a week off to go home and try to fix your marriage and I pray you do, and if you still want to transfer back to your old job, I will do the paperwork, from here.

I just don't want to jump ahead of ourselves right now; I hope you understand what I'm saying."

"I do, but I know my husband is going to be thrilled we are having a baby."

"I'm sure he will be, and I'm really happy for you."

"Thank you and I will take your advice and do just that.

I think my hardest part was telling Jan.

That I was leaving.

But I needed to do it soon, before I chickened out. She was cooking supper when I came in.

"Jan was cooking supper.

"Hey Sara, so what did the doctor say?"

"I'm pregnant, and she thinks around five months" "Oh my goodness, so how do you feel?" "I feel good, and I need to tell you something.

"The reason my husband and I are getting a divorce is because, he has always wanted a family and I have not wanted children and for

that reason he left me. And I had no idea that all the time we were fighting about having children I was pregnant, so I want to go home and put my marriage back together, and I hope you understand."

"Oh Sara, of course I understand, how could you think I wouldn't be happy for you

I think it is great that you are putting your family back together, and you are having a baby."

"Jan, thank you for all you have done for me, taking me in, and caring for me.

Chapter thirteen

Well once again my life was taking yet another turn, but this time I wasn't scared and I wasn't unhappy but just the opposite I was happy and excited, I was going home.

When I got to the airport, I rented a car because it was Saturday I knew Coy wouldn't be at work so I drove to his sister's house, the last I heard that is where Coy was staying.

I became a little nervous as I walked up to the door.

Debra opened the door with a not so welcome look on her face.

"Hi Debra, is Coy here, No Coy doesn't live here."

"Oh I have been trying his cell phone, but I think the number has been changed." I said.

"My guess is that he changed his number so you would stop calling him." She snapped.

"Will you tell me where he is, I have some very important news I need to tell him."

"Sorry don't know." Then she closed the door in my face.

Why people have to be so mean, I said to myself, as I turned toward my car.

I know over the years she never liked me and I never knew the reason, I was always nice to her. Coy said she was just a very unhappy person and didn't like anyone.

I drove to Sandra's next maybe she would know.

"Sara, I knew you would be back, I'm so happy." She said as she gave me a big hug, a very much different greeting than I had just got from my sister-n-law.

"Sandra, have you heard from Coy?"

"No I haven't in a while, is something wrong?"

"Sandra I'm pregnant, about five months.

"What are you serious?

"Yes, and I came to tell Coy, but I can't find him, and his number has been changed, and why are you looking at me like that?"

"Sara, you are five months pregnant and we are now just hearing about it.

Is that the reason you ran off to Denver? Is because you got pregnant?"

"Okay first of all. I just found out I was pregnant, and second of all. I told you why I moved to Denver.

And I really hope you are not insinuating that this baby is not Coys, because that would really hurt me coming from my own sister."

"I'm sorry of course not, you just took me by surprise that's all, oh my goodness this is great, that means you will move back home /and work out your marriage with Coy, this is awesome."

"Well that is my plan, but like I said I don't know how to get in touch with the daddy to be."

"Oh I have his address" she went into the kitchen and came back out and handed me a piece of paper with his address and new cell number on it.

"I thought you said you haven't heard from him?"

"Well I haven't, but he gave that to Scott."

"Okay wish me luck" "You don't need luck I just wish I could see the impression on his face when you tell him, he is going to be so happy."

"I know he is, I will call you later, Love you"

The closer I got to the address she had given me the more excited I became; I needed that pep talk and enthusiasm that Sandra gave me.

Just to think by this time next week I could be looking for another house to buy with my husband.

I walked up and knocked on the door, but the smile on my face was soon wiped away when a beautiful tall blond answered it.

"Can I help you" she said with a smile.

Praying I had the wrong address. I said "Is Coy here?"

"Yes just a moment" she said as she looked me up and down, my heart broke into a million pieces.

Coy, came to the door with the same look on his face as the one I got from his sister.

"What do you want?" he hurtfully said.

"Coy I need to tell you something"

"What Sara?"

"Can we go somewhere to talk please?" I asked.

He came outside closing the front door behind him. "Sara you are trying my patience what do you want?'

"I'm pregnant" I said. "Well congratulations, have a good life.

He turned to walk away. "Coy is that all you have to say?"

"What do you want me to say?"

"I thought you would be happy?"

"Sara don't even start to pretend that you are pregnant with my child, I'm not stupid"

"But it is your baby Coy" there are tests you can take, Coy, please talk to me."

"Now you listen to me Sara, I'm happy now I'm moving on with my life.

I suggest you do the same, and if by some chance you are really pregnant well I know it is not mine.

After six years of not wanting a kid, now you expect me to believe out of the blue you are having a baby. I want you to leave me alone, like I told you before we are over!

I didn't know what to say as he turned and went back into the house.

I drove around for a while trying to figure out what to do next, I felt so lost.

I didn't go back to Sandra I drove to the airport and headed toward home I was so heartbroken I knew now my marriage was really over.

I had to get over Coy and like he said move on with my life, just like he has.

I called Jan to ask her to pick me up at the airport and on the way back to her house I told her what happened.

“Sara don’t you worry about anything, I will be with you. And Sara, try not to worry about having this baby, you will be a great mother. And I’m going to help you with the baby; it’s the closest I will ever come to being a grandmother.”

Jan always had a way to make me feel better about things.

“Do you have kids Jan?” “Yes I have a son that lives in California, but he is married to his job, He is not interested in marriage most likely he never will be.”

“I’m sorry about that, Jan I don’t know what I would do without you.

“Well I’m thankful to you also Sara, I was so lonely before you came into my life and now just to think, there is going to be a baby, you have given this old woman something to look forward to in life.

I felt depressed about retiring, I didn't know what I would do, but now I'm happy."

"I'm glad, it's like god put us together." I said.

I called Sandra and told her what happened when I told Coy I'm was pregnant"

"Oh no I know he will come around I will call him and talk to him, somehow we got to make him believe this is his child"

"No Sandra, I think it's time we both realize Coy doesn't love me and he has moved on with someone else, and that our marriage is over.

I'm going to raise my baby here in Denver and Coy will not hear from me again.

So I'm asking you to please just leave Coy alone,

he has made his decision.

Chapter fourteen

THe next week I found a nice condominium for the baby and me to live...

Jan was very sorry to see me move out of her house, but I knew I needed to get settled before the baby came,

So I tried to keep her involved in everything I did.

"Hey Jan, can you please help me furnished my apartment and get it ready for our baby"

"Yes I would love too...

You don't need to ask me twice.

We had fun shopping for everything and it kept my mind off of Coy for a little while anyway.

I didn't buy anything for the baby until after my ultrasound hoping then I would find out if it was a boy or girl.

In no time my Condo looked warm and cozy, and I was starting to feel better about things, I waited for the excitement to set in about having a baby, but without Coy, I didn't want to have a baby, and I knew without love I wasn't going to be a good mother, this child needed a mother to love it.

I prayed that somewhere inside of me, I was carrying an unknown love.

That would appear once he or she was born.

I called my Dad and told him and his thinking was the same as mine and Sandra having a baby would fix everything, if only that were true.

"Dad, Coy knows and he still doesn't want me back, he said the baby wasn't his, Dad, our marriage is over.

And I'm going to accept that."

"What about if I go there and show him the light of day"

I could hear the anger in my dad's voice, "How about we just forget him, I love you dad, and I will keep you posted about the baby.

The test revealed I was having a girl. And even though I told Sandra, Coy wouldn't hear from me again it was the first thing I did.

I text Coy to tell him he was having a daughter, but I got no reply back which didn't surprise me.

The following months were very hard for me, I was so thankful I had Jan, she took care of me whenever I needed her, I was sad a lot during my pregnancy because I didn't have Coy to share things with.

Every time I would feel her kick, I would long for Coy to feel my stomach, but I kept telling myself this was his choice, and I had to move on.

Together Jan and I fixed up the baby's room it was adorable with the little mermaid

There wasn't a lot of people that knew me here so I told Jan , I did not want a baby shower, I took her with me shopping for the baby, because I didn't have a clue what the baby was going to need. Jan was a life saver for me.

And she was with me when I gave birth to my beautiful daughter.

As soon as they laid this little red baby on my chest, she took my heart away. I didn't have to worry about not loving her, I cried just to think she was my daughter.

And if Coy didn't want anything to do with her, I was determined to be the best mother and father to her I could be.

I named her after the three women I admired the most.

Jan, my mother and my sister.

Jan was so happy, when I told her I wanted my daughter to have her middle name.

Rachel Ella Marie. And I decided to call her Ella.

I had tried repeatedly to get in touch with Coy but to no avail.

Ella was a very pretty baby she had a head full of light brown hair like her dad.

Jan helped me out a lot with Ella. Thankfully because I had no idea how to be a mother.

Our life went on without Coy, I could have never imagine the love I had for this little baby, sometimes it took my breath away, I honestly didn't think I was capable of loving someone like I loved my baby girl.

Jan was a big part of her life also, she became Ella's babysitter while I worked, when I had to go away on a business trip, Jan and Ella went with me.

She loved Ella; she was the prefect grandmother to her.

My Dad came and visited me and Ella and once again he tried to talk me into moving back.

"Dad this is our home now, I miss my family but I will come and visit when Ella is older I promise."

I didn't want to go home I had come to terms that this was mine and Ella's home.

Chapter fifteen

On Jan birthday, I suggested to my boss to give her a birthday party at the office, how much it would mean to Jan.

Her son from California came, and immediately she brought him over to meet me.

"Sara this is my son Gage, and this is my new found daughter Sara" she said.

"It's nice to meet you Gage, I have heard so much about you, and I feel like I already know you."

"Well Mom never told me I had a sister, especially as beautiful as you"

"Thank you" I was almost sure my face was a thousand shades of red, not knowing what else to say, I just said excuse me and walked away. Wow what a good looking charmer I said to myself.

Jan seemed to be having a good time and I was glad, she deserved it.

"Jan, I just want to tell you happy Birthday again, and to let you know I'm going to take off and go pick up Ella"

She knew how much I didn't like to leave Ella with anyone except her when I wasn't with her.

"Oh okay dear and thank you for everything"

"You are very welcome" I said and I gave a hug.

"Hey leaving so soon, I didn't even get a dance" Gage said as he walked up to me.

"There is no music" I laughed.

"Well why is that? A party should have music and dancing,"

You seem to be enjoying yourself without those things" I said.

“Don’t mind him Sara; he is used to those parties in California”

“Okay well how tomorrow Sara, can let me take her dancing?

“I will watch Ella” Jan spoke up.

I just stood there with my mouth open trying to think of a good reason why I couldn’t but the truth was I couldn’t come up with a reason.

“Okay sounds like fun” I will see you tomorrow then say around seven o’clock?”

“Okay” seven it is, he said.

On the drive to pick up Ella, I thought about going with Gage tomorrow and I was kind of excited to be going out with him, he seem like he would be fun to hang out with.

And I could use a little fun in my life.

Gage picked me at seven sharp, he was dressed nicely, and he was the perfect gentleman.

First he took me out to eat then dancing; he kept me laughing the entire time we were together.

Long after he dropped me off, my mind stayed on Gage, he was wonderful and I would miss him when he went home, I knew he could be someone I could fall for.

But I knew I was still in love with Coy, but the pictures I had of Coy being with that Blond broke my heart every day and many nights I cried myself to sleep.

So why should I wait for a man that did not want me anymore, he has made it very plain to me that our marriage was over and we are now divorced, so why couldn't I just forget about him.

I wanted to be happy again and if I couldn't be happy with Coy, then maybe I can be happy with Gage.

I was sorry to see him leave; he was so much fun to be around and I could tell Jan, missed her son.

She had told me that he was always trying to talk her into moving to California, and it had crossed her mind to do so after she retired, but she didn't.

"Jan what is the reason you didn't move there? " Well because two very important people came into my life.

"Oh Jan, you can't let Ella and I, be the reason you don't go to be with your son, that makes me feel bad"

"Don't feel bad, I can go if I want, but I don't want to go now, end of story.

Chapter sixteen

It had been a Month after Gage went back to California, when he started calling me, at first it was just talking and laughing, but after a while it started getting serious.

I thought I was falling in love with him, we would talk every evening, and I looked forward to his calls, we even started making plans for the future together, I knew this was moving too fast, but I didn't care.

And when he asked me to come to California for a visit with his Mom, I said yes.

Ella was so always excited to be taking an airplane ride, she was five years old, and every year on her birthday I have sent Coy her picture, but I have never gotten a reply.

He was missing out on a great little girl's life, and she was the love of my life.

She loved it when I went on business trips.

She was like her mother the bright lights made her happy, she would look out the tall windows and point at all the many different colors.

Just like now looking out the plane window her eyes would get so big.

She was a joy to be around.

When we got to the airport, Gage was waiting for us; he was just as handsome as he was two years ago. He took us out to a fancy restaurant

And then a little site seeing before he took us to his home.

Gage had a beautiful house in the country, he had horses and people to take care of them, and it was amazing.

Gage had to go back to the office, so the three of us spend the evening, exploring his big house and beautiful outside gardens.

"Why does Gage live in this big house all alone with all this land if he never plans on having a family, it would make more sense if he lived in a condominium instead?

I know I have asked him the same question, his answer was, I like the country and I love having my own land to do with what I want"

The next day, we had breakfast outside on the terrace, Gage cooked the breakfast, and I was very impressed Jan told me Gage cooked when he was still living at home, a passion of his.

I was seeing a different side of Gage than what I had pictured of him. I thought maybe he was a party type guy, but he wasn't he was more a family man. I never have guessed that over the two years we had been talking, because he did talk about the party life, but I think I was starting to see that was just the way he talked.

Gage and I spend a lot of time together, which made me feel guilty taking his time from his Mother.

But she seemed so happy Gage and I was together.

We were leaving the next morning as much as I hated to leave Gage, but I had to go back to work.

Gage took me out to dinner and then a movie. In the theater during the movie, he took my hand and kissed it and whispered in my ear "I love you and I don't want you to leave tomorrow" So I leaned over and whispered in his ear "I love you and I don't want to leave, but I have too"

And again he whispered in my ear "Marry me" I laughed because I thought he was kidding.

He took my hand "let's go" I got up and we walked out very quickly as to not disturbed the people watching the movie.

We went through the theater doors laughing like school kids.

"Where are we going" I asked "Come on, you will see."

We drove for a long time it seemed but at last he pulled over, and then we walked up a hill, I was so confused.

"Gage, where are we going?" "We are almost there" he said,

"Almost there we haven't started the climb" I laughed.

When we got to the top it was absolutely breath taking I just stood there, I couldn't speak I wanted to just take in every site I could see.

"Oh Gage it's beautiful here" "Yes it is, sometimes I come here just to clear my mind of work and everything, but I have brought you here to tell you something"

"What?' I said without taking my eyes off of the splendor view below me.

"Sara, I have never been in love, not even close until I met you, you take my breath away, and I want to spend the rest of my life with you.

Sara will be my wife?"

Okay now he had my attention.

"Yes, yes I will, I said I want to spend the rest of my life with you, Gage I love you."

I could believe I had just said yes, but I felt great, I wanted to move here and I wanted to be married to Gage and to live in his beautiful house I wanted it all.

He picked me up and held me

"You have made me very happy Sara"

We decided to wait a while before we told Jan.

The plan was I would go back home and put in for a transfer, and when Gage came down in three weeks, we would take her out to dinner and then tell her, I knew she was going to be so happy.

But plans hardly ever work out.

A week after returning from California, I got a phone call from my Dad telling me my grandfather had passed away unexpectedly in his sleep, my heart was crushed not from just the fact he had died but from guilt for allowing all this time to pass and I hadn't as much as called him, but have been so consumed in my own life.

And now I would never see him again or to tell him how much I loved him.

I called my boss to let her know that my grandfather had passed away and I had to go home.

Then I called Jan, and then Gage. By that afternoon Ella and I were on the plane headed home.

Dad was waiting for us at the airport.

"Hey Dad, I gave him a hug" "Hi babe, and who is this fine looking girl, this can't be my beautiful granddaughter Ella you are too big" my dad teased her.

"I'm Ella and I'm five "she held up five fingers to prove it. "No way, you are five?" "Yep" Ella said matter-of-factly.

It was so good to see Sandra and my family again. It had been almost six years since I had seen them.

"Hi Aunt Sara, Jaden said as she gave me a big hug.

I was surprised she even remembered me.

"Oh my goodness look at you all grown up, you are beautiful." "Thank you"

"And Emma you look just like your sister, you both are beautiful"

"Yeah I know" she laughed.

"Luke can I have a hug? The last time I saw you, you were so little, now look at you"

He shyly gave me a hug.

Aunt Tina came in and gave me a hug, "where is Dana? I asked

"She is in College. Aunt Tina said proudly.

"Oh wow! Where did all the time go? The last I seen her she was what? Fifteen

My Aunt laughed, tell me about it.

My baby girl is almost twenty one years old now"

"Unbelievable, I remember this miniature bride in my wedding and now she is in college that makes me feel so old."

"I know what you mean" My Aunt said.

"So what is taking in College?" "She wants to be a school teacher" my Aunt said.

"Oh I remember when she was younger she wanted to teach school, well good for her, I'm happy to see someone's plans are working out."

"And who is this? Aunt Tina asked.

"This is Ella" "It is very nice to meet you Ella, you look just like your momma" "Thank you" Ella said.

After much catching up with the family, it was time to go to the funeral home, something I was dreading, I wanted to remember My sweet grandfather as he was the last time I seen him.

There were so many people there, people from his church where he pastored and from other churches that knew him, I couldn't believe how many people were there.

Grandfather looked so small laying there, but he seemed to be at peace almost as if he had a smile on his face, now he was with Jesus and Grandmother, so why shouldn't he being smiling,

The man that my grandfather had preached about all of his life, he got to meet him face to face.

I could just imagine the joy when he saw Jesus.

I took Ella and had a seat in the back roll because so many people were trying to view him, and as I sat there looking at everyone going up to the casket.

I couldn't believe Coy was among them.

It had been almost six years since the last time I saw him and Ella looked just like him.

I wasn't sure what to do so I just sat there, hoping he did not see me.

And then I saw Sandra talking to him, if I would have had my own car I would have left, but I had to wait for the others.

Scott came and sat with me, "How are you?"

"I'm fine, how are you?"

I asked him trying to keep the conversation going.

So we talked for a while all the time keeping my eye on Coy.

"Mom I'm tired and I'm hungry" Ella complained.

"Okay Sweetie maybe we can get grandpa's attention and leave".

And when I looked up Coy was looking straight at us, so I took Ella's hand and stood up to leave.

"Scott, please tell my Dad, I will be waiting outside for him."

Okay I will go tell him now Sara.

I took Ella to the car to wait for Dad.

So many thoughts were going through my head. Did he see Ella? Did he think she looked like him? Was he wondering if Ella was his daughter?

I was so relieved when Dad came out and we could leave.

"Sara did you See Coy?" "Yes Dad I saw him"

"He asked me how you were doing."

"That's nice" I think Dad could tell by my tone I did not want to speak about Coy around Ella. So he didn't say anything more.

After Ella was fed, and took her shower and put to bed that night did I asked Dad "exactly what did Coy say about me."

I don't know why I was so curious or why I even cared.

"He just said how Sara is, doing, I know she was close to her grandfather"

"I told him, you were doing okay, than he asked how long you would be in town and I said for a few days that was it."

Maybe it would be a good idea if he met Ella" my Dad said.

"Dad he has never wanted to meet Ella, what makes you think he does now,"

"People change Sara." "   "So I've heard. Good night Dad" "Good night sweetheart.

Chapter seventeen

I Thought about Coy and our lives we had. I wondered if he ever thought about me.

He still looked the same, and it bothered me that I still had these feelings for him, after what he did to me and our daughter.

I knew I could never forgive him, I also wondered if he remarried or if he had kids.

Was he happy now?

I tried to put him out of my mind, in a few days I would be back home to marry Gage.

The next day the funeral home was full with so many people. Everyone loved grandfather.

I noticed Coy, when we went to the grave site; He kept looking at me and Ella.

I was glad to get back into the car and head to the church.

They had a dinner at my grandfather's church in their fellowship hall.

At the dinner, Coy came up to me.

"Hi Sara, how are you?"

"I'm good thank you for coming" I was at a loss of words I didn't know what to say to him.

"Sara, can we talk?"

"Okay" I said, a little confused at what he would want to talk to me about.

"No I mean can we go somewhere later and talk, not here."

"Coy I really don't think we have anything to say to each other."

"Please Sara, here is my number, if you change your mind, please call me, I need to talk to you' He handed me a card and walked away just as Sandra walked up to me.

"What was that about?" she asked. "About five years too late" I said

"What did he say to you?" "He said he wanted to talk to me"

"What are you going to do?" Sandra asked me. I'm not sure yet."

Even though, I couldn't imagine what Coy wanted to talk to me about, unless he came to his senses and realized he was Ella's dad.

I didn't call Coy, I had too much to lose I wasn't going down that road again

But When I didn't call him, he called me, and he sounded desperate to talk to me so against my better judgment, I agreed to talk.

I was a little surprised to find out he had never married and he still lived in the house that we purchased together six years ago.

It was so beautiful here; I loved the fall colors I took it all in as I drove down the long drive that once was my home.

I walked down the long sidewall to the front door, remembering the last time I had walked to this door.

Life was so much easier back then.

Coy opened the door before I could knock.

"Thank you for coming Sara"

The house was still beautiful. It just needed a woman's touch.

So after we were seated, I didn't see the point to beat around the bush, so I just spoke my mind.

"What do you want to talk to me about?"

"Okay" he sounded nervous. "So please Sara hear me out before you say anything "

Ever since you left and then you had another man's baby, I hated you, but at the same time I have never for one moment stopped loving you, I was so mean to you, because you hurt me so bad. And then to think that you could have a baby with someone else, after denying me a child for six years, you got to understand how I felt.

But seeing you yesterday made me know I didn't care what you did to me I still love you. And you asked me why I never re married it's because of you Sara."

"Coy do you expect me to sit here and believe that after six years of you not answering my calls or responding to all the pictures I have send of our daughter.

You are asking me to believe that you still love me? Well if you do in fact still love me that is your misfortune!"

I got up to leave.

"Sara, aren't you asking me to believe something a lot harder than me loving you?

Like after six years of me begging you to have my child, and when our marriage is over, you tell me you are pregnant and expecting me to believe that it is mine? Especially since we both know you didn't even want children, and now you have a daughter.

You want me to believe that, but you can't believe that I still love you, tell me Sara, Do you still love me, or am I wasting my time."

"Coy I didn't want a child and I didn't know I was pregnant and when I found out, I will be honest with you, I still didn't want a baby.

Coy I wasn't even sure I was even capable of loving a child.

And I have never been unfaithful to you, all the time we were fighting about having a child, I was pregnant and I found out when she was born that all the time I was carrying her it was an unknown love, a love I knew nothing about, until I held this tiny little human being in my arms, I feel in love with her.

Coy, you hurt me and when I needed you the most, you left me, and I suffered knowing you were with someone else.

We both have made some bad choices in our marriage and I don't think we can fix it now."

We have a daughter now to consider.

Ella is my life and I love her more than anything in this world, and I'm not asking you to believe that you are her father, but I will tell you this, you are missing out on a great joy."

"Sara if you have any feelings for me, and if there is any way we can work this out, I will be willing to do anything, I love you Sara."

"I can't deal with this right now, Coy" and I walked out.

I knew I had to get out of there, get away from him, I could feel every plan I had made vanish.

All night I couldn't sleep, my mind was on Coy and what he said to me, was it possible that I was still in love with Coy, but I knew I loved Gage I wish I hadn't come here at last I had my life back on track and now this, I knew when I got back to Denver I would be okay.

But as fate would have it I wasn't okay, I knew I wanted to be with Coy, and that's why I started avoiding Gage's phone calls.

Coy called my cell phone constantly and left me voice messages.

I knew I was still in love with him. And I knew I had to stay away from him, I couldn't allow myself to get hurt again.

But I wasn't strong enough to listen to my sensibility, instead I listen to my emotions and the fact that I still after all these years loved Coy.

One night I called him back and we talked for a very long time that night. And continued to talk every night for the next two weeks before we decided I would move back and we would take it one day at a time with no promises.

"Coy, I would like for you to get a DNA so you know for sure that Ella is your daughter.

I don't have to do that Sara. If you say she is mine, then I believe you and I want to get to know her as soon as I can, because I have already missed these five years of her life.

Chapter eighteen

Jan, knew something was wrong, most likely by the way I was acting

I didn't know how to tell her I was leaving and breaking up with her son.

I tried to avoid her and Gage but it was pretty hard to avoid Jan.

The day she just dropped by my house made me feel so guilty, I knew I wasn't being fair to her or Gage, and I told her I was sorry I hadn't been around these last few weeks.

"Sara ever since you came back, you have been acting different, are you, and Gage okay?

Gage told me you never answer his calls."

"Jan, Ella's dad wants us to move back, he told me he still loves me, and I know I might be making the biggest mistake of my life, but I still

love him and I can't get him out of my mind as much as I have tried.

Please believe me I don't want to hurt Gage. That is why I haven't talk to him, I don't know what to tell him" by this time the tears were falling down my face.

"Sara we can't help the feelings that we have for someone, rather they are good for us or not.

But if you still love Ella's Dad, and he still loves you, maybe for Ella's sake you two can give it another try. But don't you think Gage needs to know."

"Of course you are right, I will call him tonight and tell him, thank you for not being mad at me."

"I love you and Ella and I couldn't never be mad at you for following your heart, I'm just sad that you two are leaving."

That night after Ella was in bed,

With shaking fingers I called Gage, "Hi Gage hope you wasn't already in bed."

"No I wasn't Sara. I'm so happy you called, I tried calling you several times, and I didn't want to text you about this."

"You didn't want to text me about what?

"Sara, I feel like maybe we are moving a little too fast I mean I do love you, but I want to be honest with you I just don't think right now I'm ready for a family.

When you were here I guess I just got caught up in the moment and I couldn't tell you because shorty after you got home, your grandfather passed away, I would like to still

See you when I'm in town and maybe you and my mother could come here for a visit, but I'm not ready right now for marriage."

"So are you asking for your marriage proposal back?"

"Yeah I guess so, I'm sorry" he said.

"Its fine Gage, I actually called you to tell you I'm moving back home where my family is, Ella needs to be around her grandfather, and cousins, aunts & uncle.

"And to be around her Dad?" Gage asked

"Yes also her Dad."

"Oh I think that is great and maybe now I can talk my mother into moving here with me."

"I will help you talk her into it, because I didn't want to leave her here, she needs to be with you."

"I agree, and now that you and Ella are leaving, she will consider it, I wish you all the best Sara."

"Thank you Gage, you also, good night"

"Good night Sara."

Chapter nineteen

The *next day I put in for my transfer. I spend a long of time visiting with Jan, and I didn't have to talk her into moving to California, she already had her mind made up to do so and I was glad, she was a big part of mine and Ella's life, and I didn't want to leave her here alone.*

After a tearful goodbye, we were on the road headed home.

When I phoned Coy to let him know we were on our way, he seemed very happy.

He wanted to fly out and drive back with me, but I had told him no.

I hope I wasn't making a mistake coming back.

We drove for seven hours before we got a room, this was Ella's first long car ride and

She got bored fast.

I laid down with Ella because she looked so sad.

"Mom I miss Grandma Jan, when can I see her?"

I knew this question was coming, I just didn't expect it so soon.

"Sweetie I don't know, remember Grandma Jan went on an airplane to live with Gage"

"But I want Grandma Jan" she began to weep, and it broke my heart. I hoped in time, she wouldn't miss her so badly.

I had promised Jan I would keep in touch and send her pictures of Ella.

I had made arrangements to stay with Aunt Tina, until I found a place of our own.

Ella and I both were so happy to pull into her drive way I was exhausted from the long drive and Ella was exhausted from the long ride. They both welcomed us with open arms.

"Sara I know you must be tired from your trip. But your Dad, Tami, and Michael are on their way over to see you, I hope that's Okay. "Oh yes that's fine".

Even though it hadn't been that long since we have seen each other, it was still nice to see everyone.

"Sandra had text me and she wants Ella and me to come to her house tomorrow evening for supper" I told Aunt Tina.

"That's nice. Your sister has really missed you.

I was glad when my Dad and everyone left, I just wanted to take a bath and go to bed.

After a good night's rest, I left Ella with my Aunt while I went to my job to speak to my old boss.

Coy had text me earlier to see if he could see me today, but I told him I had a lot to do

I think he understood, he just sounded disappointed.

Later at Sandra's house we had a nice visit.

Sandra and Scott seemed very happy, something I could have never imagined, but Scott had really changed, just like he said he did, I was happy for my sister.

While Sandra and I were cleaning up the supper dishes, she wanted to know all the details about Coy and I.

"Well he seemed happy I moved back, but we both agreed we are going to take things slow, get to know each other again, after all it has been six years.

"I know, I'm just so happy you are back, and I have always felt like you and Coy belonged together and now you two have a daughter."

"I'm happy to be back around my family, even though I did have a very good friend, I missed everyone here especially my sister" I said as I gave her a hug.

"I missed you too so much."

Aunt Tina and Ella really connected with each other, she took her to the park, and played games with her, she hadn't mentioned Jan in a few days.

Aunt Tina wanted to have a cookout and have the whole family over, so Coy was invited. I was glad that Coy and Ella hit it off right away. Ella was not a shy little girl; she talked to everyone, which concerned me sometimes.

She was just eating up all of this attention.

After everyone had gone home and Ella was in for the night Coy ask me to take a walk with him.

"Sara how do we do this? Do we date?"

"I'm not sure Coy, I just need some time, I have to go back to work and find Ella and myself a home"

"Sara, you and Ella have a home with me, I wish we didn't have to take things slow, I wish we could just get remarried, and you and Ella move home."

"Coy, that is not going to happen, I don't know right now what I want, but I would never do that to Ella we have to take things slow not just for our sakes but mostly for her sake"

"You are right, I didn't think about that, but I agree, I will wait as long as you want.

But tell me how you feel?' he asked.

"It's like there is something missing in my life, and I need time to figure out what that is." "I hope it's me" he said.

I'm not asking you to understand but I am asking you to please be patient."

"Sara, I told you I would wait for you for however, as long as it takes I will wait."

We walked back to my Aunts and then Coy went home.

My Aunt and Paul were at the kitchen table when I came in.

"You back so soon? " My Aunt said" "Yes we didn't walk long"

"Would you like a cup of coffee?" "Yes thank you, I didn't interrupt anything did I?"

"Oh no we were just talking about my job; I have to go out of town for a few days,

And I was just telling Tina. I'm glad you and Ella are here to keep her company,"

Paul said.

"Oh how often do you go out of town on your job?"

"Not as much as I used to, now It's maybe once a month and only for a few days.

I will be retiring next year.

"What will you do then after you retire?" "Just helping the pastor kind of taking care of the church maintenance"

"That sounds nice."

I haven't been to the church since my Dad and Tami stopped going

But my grandparents took us when we were young, Grandmother was our Sunday school teacher, I used to love to hear her tell us stories from the bible.

I want that for Ella.

"Well you and Ella should come with us Sunday." Paul said.

"Maybe we will, I don't like it that Ella has never went to church before, I want her to know about Jesus, like I did when I was growing up, my sister and I would go to Sunday school with my grandparents."

And then after my mom passed away my Dad started taking us. That is where he met Tami."

"Yes I remember that" Aunt Tina said

"Please say you will come and bring Ella"

“Okay I promise we will go Sunday with you guys. After finishing my coffee, I said Good night and went to bed.

Chapter twenty

Lying there I wondered what was wrong with me, why did I feel sad all the time, even in Denver I felt this same sadness, was it Coy. Did I feel like I was making a mistake, but I knew I loved Coy, maybe I was scared Coy would hurt me again and worst yet, that he would hurt Ella.

Because if Ella came to know him and love him as her Dad and it didn’t work out, it would be my fault for exposing her to heartache.

Ella was excited to go to church for the first time, I'm pretty sure that she was expecting something other than church.

In the foyer, I showed her a picture of his Great, Great Grandparents there was a plaque that had their names on it,

And under their name it read... "The founders of this church."

But Ella didn't seem very impressed.

Aunt Tina came up behind us, 'That's my Grandparents, but I never knew them."

"I remember you telling us, you grew up with just your mom and no family."

"Yes I loved my mom very much, and I was heartbroken when she passed away.

But I could never understand why she kept me from my grandparents and the rest of my family."

"She must have had her reasons I guess." I said.

"Yes I'm sure she did, she was a great mother to me, and I still miss her.

We went into the sanctuary to be seated. Paul was sitting on the platform.

Immediately a tear came to my eye, I missed my grandparents so much, how did I let time pass me by.

The pastor came and shook my hand and told me he was glad I was here and it was nice to meet me.

There were some people I remembered from my childhood, but a lot of new faces.

Ella went into the Sunday school class with Aunt Tina, and I sat and listened to every word the pastor was saying, it was like I was so hungry for this.

Some parts of what he was saying put a lump in my throat and I tried to hold the tears back but they were out of my control and I cried.

A lady came over to me and put her arm around me I didn't know what to do so I just laid my head on her shoulder and cried.

On the way home I told my Aunt I had felt something and I wanted to come back with them tonight.

They both seemed happy about my decision.

We went out to eat and Coy joined us. Ella and I are going to church with

Paul and My Aunt Tina, You are welcome to come if you like"

"I think I will pass, but what about tomorrow after work can I take you and Ella on a picnic?'

"A picnic? I laughed I don't think I have ever been on a Picnic in my life...

"Well good this will be our first one" Coy said.

"Okay, should I bring anything like fried children or potato salad?" I joked.

"No don't worry about bringing anything; I will take care of it."

"Are you sure not even a red checkered tablecloth?"

"Ha-ha" no it's covered." " Okay Ella I guess we are going on a picnic tomorrow"

“Yay she said, not having a clue what a picnic was unless she seen it on cartoons.

Chapter twenty one

As soon as the singers started singing, I felt God so strong I wanted to go to the altar.

But I just sat there until a man went to the altar and knelt down,

I went and I knelt down, and poured my heart out to god, I could hear my Aunt beside me and other people were around.

But it didn't matter as far as I was concerned it was just me and god.

I told God I was sorry for every sin I had ever did in my life, but it was hard to talk because of the power of God and the tears.

Someone asked me if I wanted to stand, so they helped me to my feet and I raised my arms and praised god, it was so overwhelming and it seem to go for a long time, I wanted to stop so I could tell someone, that God just gave me the holy ghost I just had to tell someone, I could hear people around me shouting.

When I opened my eyes some people were running around the church and some were shouting, this feeling was magnificent, something I has never in my life experienced.

Aunt Tina was hugging me and we both were crying, I looked around for Ella to make sure she wasn't scared she was lying on the pew asleep someone had covered her with a blanket.

That night I found what was missing in my life, it was Jesus.

After church I was baptized in the name Of Jesus Christ. And they told me Jesus washed all my sins away. I felt great

I couldn't wait to tell Coy and Sandra.

The next day that is what I did, I showed up at Sandra's house unexpected. on my lunch break.

"Sara, hey come in, what's up?"

"Oh Sandra I'm sorry I didn't call first, but I had to tell you something,

"Last night I went to church with Aunt Tina and Paul and guess what?

"I don't know" she said.

"God gave me the Holy Ghost and I was baptized, oh Sandra it was so wonderful.

"Well I'm happy for you" she looked at me like she didn't know what to say,

Sandra knew about the gift of the Holy Ghost because we both heard it when we were young.

But up until last night I had no idea what it was.

"Sara I'm happy that you are happy" "Oh I'm so happy" I said,

I'm meeting Coy, he is taking Ella and me on a picnic, so I'm going to tell him but I just wanted you to be the first to know.

And to ask you please come to church with me."

We will see" she said.

But everybody knows what that means I thought.

Coy asked me to meet him at the park.

I waited until we were seated on a blanket in front of a lake to tell him about my experience last night.

Ella was tossing rocks into the water so I took this opportunity to tell Coy.

"Coy last night at church God filled me with Holy Ghost and then after church I was baptized, and I found what I was looking for, I feel so happy, I wanted to share it with you and to tell you

it's very real and it's amazing."

"Wow, I have never understood your grandparents or your Aunt's religion, but I must be honest, you seemed to be different today."

"I am different." I told him.

"Oh Coy I really am, for the first time in my life, I feel peace."

"Sara I'm happy for you, but please understand this doesn't mean I buy into all of this holy ghost and stuff, I went to church when I was a teenager, but I mostly went because I love to play baseball, and they had a team, but on occasions I would listen to the preaching and I will go as far to say I was touched, but just because this is good for you doesn't mean it is good for me'.

"Oh Coy It is good for everybody."

"Well I hope it doesn't change your feelings for me, I'm not saying I won't ever go to church with you and Ella, because if that is what you want, then I will go, I'm just asking you not to expect me to change also, that's all I'm saying."

"Okay that is fair, because I know you don't understand, but you need to know this is my life style now, Ella and I will be going to church and living from now on for God."

After our picnic of pizza and drinks were over. I went to tell my Dad about church and what happened,

Dad knew all about the holy ghost so did Tami, they met in church and we went every service growing up, so they both were very happy for me and promised me they would come soon. I left there walking on cloud nine. It really is joy unspeakable just like the song says.

Every church service just got better for me I loved it, and Coy kept his word he did come to church every service, and I could tell when the power of God was moving, he was fighting back tears, I knew sooner or later if he kept coming, he would lose the fight.

The three of us spend a lot of time together, it was fun, Coy never asked me to go anywhere against my belief and I appreciated that from him.

Chapter twenty two

T*He day came when I told my boss I could no longer go out of town, so he told* *me, that was fine because he needed me more at home base he would assign me jobs at the office.*

Ella loved school, and I had found a nice apartment not far from the school, everything was going good...

Coy and I got involved with things at the church; there seem to be always something going on.

Coy also was becoming friends with some of the guys that went there.

And one Sunday night, Coy made his way to the altar

I stood there with tears running down my face; God is so awesome, all the men were praying with him. And before church

Was over he stood and told everyone. He was going to get the Holy Ghost and he wanted to change his life. Everyone cheered.

The following week he was baptized and he came up from the water speaking in tongues.

Three months later Coy called me at work to ask if he could pick Ella up from School.

I told him that was fine, Coy had changed so much, he was so different, and I feel in love with him all over again.

When I walked in the door, I was so surprised to see them both dressed up, Coy in his suit...

"What is all this about?"

"Mom have a seat please we have a surprise for you, Ella was so excited about whatever the surprise was.

So I took my seat while she ran into her room, a moment later she came and handed me an envelope, with drawings all over it and I was pretty sure the artist was a six year old.

I opened it and there was a note that read..."

Don't fix supper tonight, because we are taking you to your favorite restaurant."

I looked at Coy who had a big smile on his face.

"A poet" I said.

"Okay mom go get dressed"   "Okay" "Hurry mom"   "Okay I will hurry"

All the time I was getting dressed I could hear Ella bubbling with excitement.

At the restaurant Ella said "Mom you can't have no dessert here Okay"

"Okay: I said   "Are you done eating mom?"

"Yes I'm all done" "Okay close your eyes"

I closed my eyes, she handed me another envelope and as I looked at it I could see by the same artist

The note read "Roses are red violets are blue, right after we have ice cream we have another surprise for you."

"Come on mom "Ella took my hand, on the way out the door I said to Coy, "Is this surprise from Ella or you?"

He just laughed.

So we sat at the little parlor and had ice cream. After that they took me to the beach where I discovered a bench was set up, and as I walked behind Ella, who was in a hurry to get there.

I could see roses Ella, came running back to me, "Mom these are for you" "Wow, thank you, they are beautiful, are these from you or Coy?' I asked.

"They are from both off us" Ella informed me.

I was told to sit on the bench then Ella said "I'm going right over there but don't worry mom I won't get close to the water Okay." "Okay, thank you"

Coy came and sat next to me. "Does any of this look familiar?"

"Yes, the restaurant and the ice cream parlor, and it was here. At the end of the night you asked me to marry you."

Coy got down on his knee in front of me and I could hear Ella giggling.

"Sara, I love you with all of my heat, will you marry me again?"

"Yes, I will marry you again.

He picked me up and yelled to Ella. "She said yes"

Ella came running toward us. "We did it sweetheart, thanks for all your help, I couldn't have done it without you" "I know because I helped you ""yes you did." Coy told her.

The following Sunday, we talked to our pastor, about being married

We both agreed we wanted a private ceremony with just the pastor and his wife and our immediate family.

We did t counseling with our pastor, before we announced our plans to remarry.

We told my Dad first, he was thrilled to say the least.

Then we told Sandra and Scott, we invited them to supper one night.

"Sandra, Coy, and I are getting remarried, and I want you to stand up with me, it will be a very small ceremony"

"Yes I would love to, I'm so happy for the two of you."

"And Scott, I would like for you to stand up with me" Coy said to Scott.

"Sure I will, congratulations you two"

"So have you set a date yet" Sandra asked.

"Yes we are getting married in October" "Oh that will be nice,"

"Yeah and that is good timing because Sandra and I are taking the kids on a small vacation, before Jaden goes off to college" Scott said. "Oh that is good, you two deserve a vacation. I'm so happy you guys get to go on one"

"I'm so looking forward to it, the kids never get to go anywhere really, so it will be fun for them, they are excited."

"Where are you taking them?" I asked.

"We are taking them where every kid wants to go

"Disney land?"

"Oh wow lucky kids" Coy said "Honey I want to go to Disney land on our honeymoon

He joked.

"Maybe next year "I said.

Chapter twenty three

Te day of our wedding was cold and raining, I had asked Coy if we could fly to Denver on our honeymoon and he agreed just for a few days. We stood in front of our pastor, and read each other our vows that we had written. Coy said his first...

"Sara almost six years ago I made the biggest mistake of my life when I let you slip away from me, you are a million prayers I have prayed, and you are a million tears I have cried.

God in all of his mercy gave you back to me. And to me you are a treasure from God and I promise to always treat you as my treasure. When God gave you back to me, you lead me to him, I love you and Ella with my whole heart and I will prove that love to both of you every day and I will thank God every day for you both.

After wiping my tears I read mine.

"Coy, I know as long as we service God together, we will stay together, because the closer we get to him, the closer we will become, I love you, and I will do my best to be the wife that God has intended me to be.

After the service, we all went out to Dinner, we had a good time.

After giving Ella many kisses and hugs bye, Coy, and I drove to the airport.

Aunt Tina was happy to be taking care of Ella while we were gone.

I had made reservations at the same hotel across from the little park, I had went to years ago when My life was falling apart, but now God has put my life back together. After we checked into our room we went to the park and sat on the same bench, and took in all the beauty of the fall color as Coy held my hand.

And I thanked God for blessing me and for loving me, and for putting my marriage back together.

We took a walk down town to the little shops, I loved the cool autumn, and there was just a certain fragrance in the air.

I wasn't ready to go back home, but I did miss Ella.

Before we left we walked back to the park, and we watched as couples walked hand in hand and my mind went back to when I sat on this same bench with a broken heart and I watched as couples walked by me hand in hand and how much I missed Coy.

And here I was again only things were so much different; I had so much to be thankful for.

Coy promised me next fall we would come back and spend two weeks here with Ella if I wanted.

"Oh Coy, I would love that.

Chapter Twenty four

Mom I need another box for all my things" Ella was saying as we packed up our belongings for our move to Coy's house.

"Okay here you go" I loved the excitement she had about the move I was also happy we didn't have to put her into a different school.

"Hey I have room for a few more items in the truck than I will have to come back for the rest." Okay Coy, take these next, we will finish up here while you are gone."

At last at the end of the day, everything had been moved, the apartment was spotless, and the keys had been returned.

"How about we have Pizza for supper? "Yay" Ella said without taking her eyes from the hand held game she was playing.

"That's sounds good to me "I said, all I wanted was a shower and rest.

It was so nice to have this big house to redecorate the way I wanted to, this was my first home, and

I really liked it, for some reason it seemed smaller than before.

We decided to replace everything and start from new.

After work and on weekends, we were either painting or looking for furniture.

I wasn't a cook, in fact I hated to cook, but I was making myself learn and starting to enjoy it, now that I knew what I was doing

We invited our family over for thanksgiving, and this would be my first attempt to cook a big meal, we also invited Debra, Cody's sister but she said she was going out of town with friends.

Everything went very well, even though Sandra and Tami had to help me with a few things.

But I made it through my first thanksgiving, and everyone enjoyed themselves.

Usually after thanksgiving I would feel down, but now I didn't have time to feel down there was always something going on at church.

We went to church gatherings with the other couples once a month,

Ella loved Sunday school, she got to go with her class to museums and roller skating parties, I was happy she liked church so much and was learning about Jesus.

We had a Christmas Eve gathering at our house, I invited a few people from our church, and also the pastor and his wife, I wanted to expose them to my family.

I saw my Dad and the pastor in a long conversation, and I hoped my plan was working.

I could tell Sandra was happy I was home because she got to get out of the house more and spend time with us. She still hadn't come to church yet, but I wasn't giving up, I knew she had to feel left out, because now Dad and Tami went every service and Michael had promised me he would come.

I loved being around church people, they had such a sweet spirit about them and they were so much fun, during the games Sandra was laughing so hard it was so good to see her feel involved.

Everyone had to go home early because they knew their kids would have them up at four am. To open gifts.

This would be Ella's first Christmas with her Dad But also her first Christmas without Jan.

Coy woke me up at six am. "Hey why isn't our daughter up?" "I don't know I laughed

"Well I'm waking her up" Coy jumped out of bed.

After getting dressed I went into Ella's room where I found Coy very softly saying

"Ella, its Christmas gets up or I'm going to open all of your gifts"

I could see the smile on Ella's face, Then she jumped up and ran down the stairs with Coy right behind her. By midmorning I was ready for a nap.

Our living room looked like Christmas had exploded in it.

Chapter twenty five

THe summer was hot, but it didn't stop Ella and me from working in our yard and garden.

One day as we were doing that, a big truck pulled into our drive to unload some building material, I was sure they had the wrong address; Coy came home as they were unloading it.

"What are you building?" I said as I came to stand beside him while he watched them take the lumber out of the truck I wonder because it wasn't that much material.

"I promised a certain someone that when summer got here we was going to build something"

"A treehouse" Ella screamed. "That's right, you didn't forget did you?" Coy asked her.

"No way"

So that weekend I bit my nails as I watched them build their treehouse, wishing Sandra and her family were here to keep me occupied, but they were enjoying their much needed vacation.

I called dad and invited him and Tami over for a cookout and to watch coy try to build a treehouse, I liked be around Tami now that she was back in church, we had a lot to talk about.

Tami had been raised in this church, when my grandfather was the pastor here.

We had a good time watching the men try to build the treehouse, it was quite funny, I think they scratched their heads and looked at the instructions more than anything.

Ella had lost interest and went to her room with her friend from next door.

When our food was done and they took a break to eat, I asked Coy if I should call in reinforcements. "Yes call Paul" he said with down casted eyes.

Two hours after Paul arrived the treehouse was open for business.

And Ella loved it.

That night as I laid in bed I thought about how my life has changed, at one time my career was my top priority, but now God and my family are my top priority, I was happy I was surrounded by my family who would have thought this was what I had always needed in my life.

I had cleaned all day and did all the laundry getting ready for the week, sorry our weekend was over.

After we were done praying Coy and Ella had gone to bed.

I was just about to take my bath before I went to bed, When the phone rang, trying to get it before it woke Coy up, I couldn't imagine who would be calling us this late.

But that call would change everyone's lives forever.

Chapter twenty six

Sara, it's Dad, I just received a phone call and Sandra was involved in an accident they sounded like it was pretty bad, even though they didn't say that, Michael is on the phone now getting our plane tickets, it's over six hundred miles from here" I could hear Dad's voice starting to break.

I looked up to see Coy standing in front me.

"Dad, we don't know that it was bad, so let's not jump to conclusions Okay, as far as we know no one was hurt, I need you to stay calm"

"I'm trying Sara, but they are so far away" "But by plane you will be there in no time, I told him.

Have you called Aunt Tina?" " No, you are the only one." " Okay I will call her and we will be there as soon as we can" After he gave me the state, city and address to the hospital we hung up.

Coy was talking to the pastor on the phone.

So I called Aunt Tina. After telling her everything that Dad had told me, and giving her the information, she said they would leave soon.

"Sara I'm taking Ella to the Pastor's house, you need to call the airport to get our tickets'

"Okay"

As he was walking out the door with Ella he stopped and looked at me.

"Sara I need you to take the advice you just gave your dad, I need you to stay positive, and know God is in control."

"I'm trying and I know he is in control, hurry back please."

After getting our tickets, I quickly got dressed and threw some things in a suitcase for the two of us.

I tried my best to hold the tears in while I was waiting for Coy to return, but I couldn't.

I prayed to God that this family was okay and to keep his hand on them, on all of us.

When we were finally on the plane, my mind kept playing over and over questions, why were they traveling on these roads this late? They should have been in a hotel, sleeping what changed their plans? Did Scott fall asleep at the wheel? How are the children Are they hurt?

Every one of them was so happy to be going on this vacation, why did this have to happen?

I just started crying. Coy put his arm around me. Sara we don't know, all of this worry could be for nothing.

"Let's remember our memory verse."

"Be strong and of a good courage, fear not, nor be afraid of them for the lord thy God, it is he that doth go with thee, he will not fail thee nor forsake thee."

God said he is our refuge and strength, a very present help in trouble.

Sara we have to keep our trust in Jesus. "I know, Coy I'm trying not to be scared.

Once we got to the airport, we had to wait to rent a car, I didn't think I had the tolerance to wait for a rental car, I was eager to get to the hospital, I needed to be with my sister and her family.

"Okay come on, let's get a cab" Coy took my hand and led me outside of the airport where cabs were lined up waiting for passengers.

It wasn't far to the hospital I text Michael to ask him where we should go when we got there; He said he would be waiting outside for us.

When the driver dropped us off at the front entrance We could see Michael, but as I got closer my stomach stated turning It felt like it was coming up into my chest, I seen him crying, so I almost ran to him, "Michael tell me" I demanded.

"She is gone, Sandra is gone" he cried and his whole body was shaking, if Coy had not been holding me up I would have fell.

"No she can't be, you are mistaking, take me to Dad, Michael you are wrong!" I cried.

"Coy take me to my father, I have to see Sandra"

Coy held me as we followed Michael down the long hallway I could see his shoulders shaking.

We walked into the room. Dad was sitting on a couch with his head down, Tami was trying to comfort him, and he looked like he had aged since I saw him just yesterday.

I went to him and sat next to him. "Dad how is Sandra?' He looked from me to Michael

"Sara, your sister didn't make it" he cried "Can I see her, I want to see her"

Coy took me out of the room. "Sara we have to be strong for your Dad"

"I can't. I want to see Sandra" I pleated.

My mind could not comprehend what they were telling me, I knew she had died but it was like I couldn't accept that until I saw her.

A doctor came in the room and was talking to us, Aunt Tina and Paul and our pastor had arrived by this time.

The doctor told us that Sandra had died on impact, she did not suffer, Scott died on the transport to the hospital, the children were expected to have a complete recovery, and Emma was in surgery but was also expected to have a complete recovery.

Our pastor asked that we all hold hands, we did, and he prayed.

Everyone in the room was crying, the hurt was too deep, how could they be gone.

My sister was a part of me, I needed her.

After the Doctor left, Aunt Tina Pulled us to the side so Dad couldn't over hear us talk.

"Right now there are three children that are going to need us, and we have to be strong for them.

And that is going to mean no tears in front of them, we are the adults and even though our pain is great, we have to put on a Front, when we are with them, because they are children and have just lost both of their parents, we have God on our side, and he will Get us through this. I have asked Paul to call Scott's grandmother And Aunts to tell them what has happened.

Aunt Tina took me in her arms and held me while we both cried. I knew that my Aunt was not a stranger to this kind of Heartbreak and pain. When I had stopped crying, she told me And Coy to go be with Jaden. She went to be with Luke.

"Michael right now Emma is still in surgery.

Can you go see if you can find out anything please?"

Pastor went into each room and prayed for them.

Chapter twenty seven

W*hen we walked into Jaden's room, as hard as I tried*

I couldn't hold back the tears, I was thankful she

Was sleeping and couldn't see me, her hand was in a bandage,

But it was her beautiful face that was so swollen and bruised.

Both of her eyes were black and red swollen.

We sat beside her bed, and I laid my head on Cody's shoulder I couldn't stop my tears, I cried for my sister.

After only being there a few minutes, the nurse came in and asked us who we were and to let us know the doctor would be in soon.

We walked out in the hall way just outside her door to wait for him.

I saw a doctor walking toward us looking at his chart as he walked.

"Hello, I'm Doctor Jenkins, I'm treating Jaden, and you are?"

"I'm Sara, Jaden's aunt and this is her Uncle Coy"

"First of all I want to say how very sorry I am for your lost."

"Thank you" I said.

"Jaden is a very lucky young lady, there are no broken bone, her

Hand has seven stitches, and she has some bruising, but nothing

That time will not heal. Thank goodness she was wearing her seatbelt, or this conversation could be going a whole different way."

"Thank You Doctor Jenkins, Can you tell us about Emma, Jaden's sister, is she out of surgery yet?"

"I will go find out for you" As he turned to leave I had to ask him another question.

"Can you tell us what happened?" He turned and looked at me.

"I do know the two officers are still here if you would like to talk to them"

"I would, thank you" "If you follower me I will get them for you"

He took us to a small room. "I will tell the officers you are here and I will check on Emma for you." Then he left.

"Sara are you sure, you are up to this?" "Yes Coy I want to know"

But when I saw the two police men, I wasn't sure anymore.

"Hi I'm office Williams and this is Officer Banks"

"Hi I'm Coy and this is my wife Sara, her sister was involved in the accident last night.

"Hi Ma'am, we are truly sorry for your loss"

"Can you tell me what happened?" I asked.

"We were the first to arrive on the scene and as of right now as far as we can tell, because the accident is still under investigation.

It was very foggy, apparently there was a pickup truck following too close to your sister's van, hitting the van and knocking it into oncoming traffic, the van in which your sister was a passenger in was hit head- on by a another truck.

Ma'am I know this won't help, but your sister was thrown from *the van and died on impact, she didn't suffer, for some reason she was not wearing a seatbelt, but in this case, a seatbelt would have served no purpose."*

After thanking the officers, we went back into Jaden's room.

We sat for hours Jaden only opened her eyes a few minutes at a time, and I would try to talk to her, but she would just turn her face away, She did drink some water for the nurse and one time she said "I just want to sleep please" It was night time and the nurse had just given her something to help her sleep and said she would be out for a while.

"Can I leave you my cell number so you can call me, when she wakes up?"

"Yes dear I will call you as soon as she is a wake, and if you like I can put a bed in her room so you can rest." "Thank you very much; I might want to do just that in a few hours"

"Coy can we go back into the chapel I want to pray"

When we got to the Chapel the pastor and Aunt Tina and Paul were there praying as well, it gave me comfort to have my pastor here.

"When we went back into the room where my dad was, he was standing looking out the window.

Tami came and gave me a hug. "How are you doing Sara?" "will as I can, I guess"

"I'm going to take your dad to the hotel just right down the street so he can rest, I'm worried about him"   "Okay that is a good idea" I told her.

"Coy you should just take Michael and go get a room. We have all been up for hours"

"I'm not leaving you"   he said.

"I will rest in Jaden's room, I promise."

He finally agreed.

After everyone went to the hotel, I went to Jaden's room; the nurse had already put a bed in the room for me

I sat in the chair and watched Jaden sleep.

I was exhausted, but knew I would not sleep; I went out into the hall and called Aunt Tina to see if she had heard any news on Emma.

She told me she would be right up.

"You look very tired" Aunt Tina said... "So do you" I said.

"Emma is out of surgery and doing well.

They will let us know as soon as she is out of recovery.

Paul went and got a room but I'm staying here

"I'm staying here also they put a bed in Jaden's room for me"

"They are keeping Luke pretty much out of it; I'm just going to sit with him just in case he wakes up and finds no one there with him.

They also put a bed in his room for me, but I doubt I use it."

As we were speaking, a nurse informed us, Emma was in her room and we could go in. our Pastor went in with us to pray for her.

She looked so small. We walked up to her bed and Aunt Tina started rubbing her hand.

She opened her eyes and looked at us.

"Momma" she cried. And held her hand out to me.

I bend down and took her in my arms.

I couldn't stop the tears, I held her until she fell back to sleep.

When I stood back up, I saw Aunt Tina drying her eyes.

"How are we going to get thought this, Aunt Tina?"

"God will help us.

The next day, we all left the hospital to go home.

We had to make the arrangements for the funerals.

It was the worst days of our lives. I didn't think I would ever be happy again, I didn't think the tears would ever stop. My pastor had send word ahead for the church to have everything ready; everyone went out of their way to help out with everything. They took care of all of the food but most of all I appreciated their prayers.

Chapter twenty eight

It was so hard to pick out a casket for my sister, but I knew my dad couldn't do it. So Coy and I did all the details, Sandra and Scott was already back in our home state, we were told by the funeral director, they both would have closed caskets.

I didn't think I had no more tears left to cry.

The services were sad, everyone tried to say kind words, and we were very appreciative of that.

As much as I hated leaving Ella again, I felt like I needed to get back to the hospital to be with the kids, almost like now I knew I had to step into Sandra's shoes, because I know that is what she would have wanted.

Right after the services and spending some time with my daughter, Aunt Tina and I went back to the hospital. Everyday Luke and Emma was getting better

The whole family was there when Emma woke up, it had been three weeks since the accident, and we all were just going through the motions of everyday living, just trying to survive without breaking down every other minute,

Jaden went into a shell, she didn't talk much, and she just made a fuss over her siblings she wanted to take care of them all by herself.

Even though Jaden had been released from the hospital   she would not go to my house and stay

It was when Luke was released that Jaden would agree to go home.

I knew Jaden was mothering Luke.

It was almost like she felt guilt about her parents, my heart went out to her, and she was so young to carry such a burden.

Emma and I were the only ones left at the hospital, because everyone had to get back to their jobs but they called daily to check on Emma.

She was adjusting well with everything that happened and it was such a happy bright sunny day, the day we walked out of the hospital to go home.

When we pulled in our driveway, there was a big banner that readied "Welcome home Emma" all the family was there and so happy to see this young lady.

But still sadness hung in the air, and all three children had a lonely look in their eyes, everyone's lives had changed, and I knew only God and time could heal us.

I tried to make a home for the kids and to take their minds off of everything   but it was on those sad occasions when Luke would accidentally call me mom, then our house would get that sad feeling in it.

It broke my heart, I missed Sandra so much, and I could only imaging the hurt these three children were in.

I took a year off my job to stay home and care for the kids, Jaden was a big help.

Time went by and we saw the children smile or laugh again.

But not Jaden so after a year, we thought it was best that Jaden continued her plans to go to college

But she refused to even discuss it.

"Jaden you know your mother was so happy that you were going to college, this is what she would have wanted."

"No! I won't go." She sounded so sad.

"But tell me why? Because you know Coy and I will take good care of Emma and Luke.

Honey we don't want you to worry about that," I said.

"Aunt Sara, you just don't understand."

"Then Jaden talk to me, help me to understand.

"I can't" she started to cry.

"Sweetie, I haven't asked you about the accident before, because I know how painful it is for you to talk about it, but if you ever want to talk about it, you can, it will be okay."

"I don't want to." She cried. "Okay, you don't have to" I put my arms around just to feel her body stiffing up like always

So I just held her, trying to comforter her, but Jaden refused to be comforted.

Coy and I talked about it and we both agreed I wouldn't go back to work for a few years, we both felt like the kids needed me home.

Jaden did go to church with the family, but she would only sat there with her head down, I was really becoming concerned about her.

My pastor tried talking to her, but she wouldn't open up to him, she didn't leave the house other than to go to church.

Coy and I felt if only we could get her to attend collage it would help her to take her mind off of everything.

Emma was always kind of quiet, and kept to herself, but she did like going to go to church.

She had met a friend there, and once I seen her laughing, it was so good to hear her laugh again

Luke seemed to be adjusting well.

I had noticed he wanted to spend a lot of time with Coy.

It was just Jaden that I was worried about most.

Dad and Michael started spending a lot of time at our house bonding with the children.

I knew Dad was in his own personal misery missing Sandra so.

It was good for him to be around his grandchildren.

It was on one of those nights after Dad and Michael left, that I found out just how heavy of a burden Jaden was carrying.

She had went upstairs to bed as soon as Dad left, and after straightening the kitchen, I went up, just as I was getting ready for bed, I heard something that sounded like crying, thinking it may be Ella having a bad dream, I went to investigate

Finding her sleeping soundly, I continued down the hall to Emma and Jaden's room I heard crying, I softly knocked, when no answer came, I went inside.

Emma was spending the night at her friend's so I knew it must be Jaden Crying.

I sat on the edge of her bed, and began to stroke her hair.

"Jaden sweetie, would you like to talk about it?"

"No, Aunt Sara, I can't." She said pitifully.

"I know you miss your mom and Dad, and if I could I would take your hurt away, but I can't. But Jesus can help you; he can heal your broken heart if you could just give it all to him."

"Why would Jesus help me do anything? It was my fault my mother is dead if anything God blames me. She cried

"Oh Jaden, honey it's not your fault " I couldn't believe this young girl thought she was the cause of her mother's death, what a heavy burden.

"You don't understand, you weren't there, you don't know!" she cried.

"Jaden please tell me, so I can understand and help you, please Jaden talk to me." I pleaded.

Thought many tears she began.

"Mom and Dad had decided to drive all the way home instead of stopping at a hotel for the night like they had planned, and I was so mad, because I wanted to stop, so I wasn't speaking to either of them.

And then to top it all off, mom had insisted on stopping at a grocery store and buying food. Because she told Dad it would be so much cheaper than going through a fast food place, because they had spent so much money on the vacation all ready. And Dad agreed.

So dad stopped at a stupid grocery store, mom tried to get me to go inside the store with her, but I was so mad at her I said no and I stayed in the car.

So after we got back on the road, Mom started making sandwiches for us, and when she offered mine, I said I didn't want one.

She tried to tell me, she was sorry that we couldn't afford to stop at a hotel, but I didn't care what she said, I was still mad at her.

She continued to make the sandwiches and she handed Emma one, Emma was sitting behind Dad, and Luke was sitting in his booster seat, I was sitting behind Mom, after she handed Luke his, she told me to get Luke a drink out of his bag, but I just pretended like I didn't hear her I just turned my face toward the window,

So she took her seat belt off and turned around to get Luke's drink and I felt the blow from behind us, and that's all I remember, the Doctor said my head hit the back of the front seat and it knocked me out before we hit the truck So don't you see? Dad's side was hit the hardest, so if she would have been wearing her seat belt, she wouldn't have died" she was crying so hard, my heart was being tore from my chest, to hear the details of my sister's death.

"Jaden, Listen to me. Stop crying and listen to me please."

I knew I had to calm her somehow.

"It's not your fault it just happened, if she would have had her seat belt on, she still wouldn't have made it, it wouldn't have matter if she would

have had her seat belt on. The police officer told me that. Do you hear me, it just happened and it's no one's fault

She started to calm down some so I continued.

It's sad that you were mad at your parents, but if they were here right now, they would tell you the same thing. Jaden they loved you and it would break their hearts to know you blame yourself and are hurting like this.

Honey all teenagers get mad at their parents, it's okay, you can't spend the rest of your life beating yourself up over it."

"I never told them I'm sorry" she cried.

"Okay then let's do that now." I took her hand and we knelt down beside her bed and I told her just to talk to them and tell them.

I just wanted her to ease some of the burden she was carrying.

She cried and she told them how sorry she was and how much she loved and missed them.

And I prayed to God for help for Jaden to give me knowledge to help her.

I stayed with her until she fell asleep, she looked so much better after she talked out everything that had been weighting her down, she had a horrible guilt, now hopefully it was gone for now anyway.

If she would only turn to God,

And allow him to fix her broken heart.

Chapter twenty nine

But Jaden didn't change. But got a whole lot worst, she started refusing to go to church with us, she started staying out late, she dyed her hair bright red, I knew she was acting out because of the hurt, just like her dad did when he lost his dad, Aunt Tina had told me all about it, when I talk to her about Jaden, I was at the end, I didn't know how to help her, she wouldn't talk to me.

If only we could convince her to go to college to get on with her life, because the path she was on now was a bad one.

I just wanted to get her away from the group she had started to hang out with.

My pastor told me just to give her time, and I was trying very hard, but I felt like I had my hands full.

The other kids were doing really well, they loved church.

Emma was involved in a lot of thing at church they made friends.

She and Luke were doing very well in school.

I knew Jaden was hurting, and I wanted to help her, but all I could do was pray for her.

We gave her everything she needed, we bought her a car, which now I regret doing.

Because she stayed out all night, even though she wasn't a kid anymore, it didn't stop me from worrying about her

One nigh I waited up for Jaden to come home from one of her nights out and I was getting more upset as the minutes passed. This had to stop.

As soon as she walked in and seen me standing there, her attitude went bad.

"What are you doing up?" she looked shocked to see me.

"Jaden it is three in the morning, where have you been?"

"Are you kidding me" I'm twenty years old, I don't have to answer to you, but if you must know, Out"

"I'm aware you have been out Jaden, sit down, we need to talk." I demanded.

"Can't this wait, I'm tired" "No this cannot wait Sit!"

"Fine but can you made it quick" she said as she sat down.

"Jaden we have been very patient with you but it has been almost two years, and this kind of

behaver from you ,has got to stop now, I want to make you an appointment to talk to someone. "

"No, I'm not going and talking to no one!" She got up to leave.

"Jaden, this conversation is not over" "Aunt Sara, you may look like my mother, but you are not! Good night." And she marched upstairs.

I stayed up for a while. My mind was racing at what to do next.

When I did finally did go to bed, I just laid there and cried, I felt like I had let my sister down.

Dad and Tami came over every Friday evening to give Coy and I time to ourselves and this week I needed it.

So I decided to talk to my dad about Jaden.

"Dad, I don't know what to do about Jaden anymore, she is staying out later, and later, we

don't know who she is with. Or what she is doing? I need your help"

"I will talk to her, she is almost twenty years old it's time she gets a job and moves out of your house, have you told her that?

No I can't, what would Sandra think of me if I made her daughter leave.'

"She can stay with me," He said. "I will straighten her out, she is not a teenager, but a grown woman, it's time she starts acting that way. And it's time for you to stop treating her like a teenager, I know she is your sister's daughter and you have guilt. But can't you see this is not good for you and it's certainly not good for Jaden."

"I know you are right dad, just talk to her maybe you will have better luck with her than I did."

"Sara, you ready?" Coy came in the room.

"Yes, see you later Dad, we won't be out long"

"Take your time, we will be fine."

Coy and I had a nice dinner then we went to the lake just to walk and enjoy the quietness

We were so thrilled when Emma expressed an interest in going to Midwest Apostolic Bible College next year.

I talked to Coy about the conversation I had with Jaden the other night and also what my dad told me.

"Sara I agree with your dad, I mean right now we have a dilemma, and Jaden needs to be independent because if she was, then it would be good for her and us.

I know the struggles life has to offer but this situation at home has to change not only is it not good for you, because I know you worry all the time about her, but it's not good for the other kids either.

Especially Emma right now, she is at that vulnerable age and she is doing well in church I don't want her older sister being a bad influence around her."

"Okay so we should talk to her again and give a time to have a job or go to college and next year she has to move out if she is not in college." I said.

"Right I think that would be best for everyone" Coy said.

I felt better now after talking to my dad and Coy, I didn't feel guilty anymore but I had some hope now.

Chapter thirty

The next morning when Jaden got ready to leave, Coy stopped her.

"Jaden before you leave Sara and I would like to talk to you"

"Are you kidding? Aunt Sara already had that talk with me, and I'm late."

"Jaden, we are going to have a talk before you leave this house and it will be up to you on how long it will take"

"I'm not a child and I would appreciate it if you two would stop treating me like one."

I don't want to talk, See ya" she walked out the door, with Coy right behind her.

"You don't want to be treated like a child and yet that is exactly how you are acting."

Jaden just kept walking to her car.

Coy yelled at her.

"Your things will not be here after you leave, so don't bother to come back, the locks will be changed.

She just threw her hand up in the air, got into her car, and drove away.

Coy got his keys and walked toward his truck, "Where are you going?" I asked

"To the hardware store I will be right back, pack her things please."

I was so glad Emma and Luke was not at home to hear this and Ella was in the treehouse playing with her friend.

I knew I had to stand with my husband with the decision he just made to kick her out

But it was breaking my heart, "I'm sorry Sandra" I whispered

I packed her things up, I prayed Jaden would see that we were serious and come home and change her ways.

She was such a smart beautiful girl I hated to see her throwing her life away.

After Coy came home, he started changing all the locks, he wasn't playing around.

"Coy what are we going to do with her things?"

"Your dad said to bring her things to his house"

"You called dad what did he say? He said it was about time we took a stand with her." We put her things into the truck and Coy took them to my dad's

Around two am, we were in bed when we heard Jaden trying to unlock the door.

She didn't believe Coy would do it apparently.

"Coy should I go tell her to go to her grandfather's?"

"No he said he has texted her, so she knows"

My heart ached, I just wanted to hold her to make everything better, but I knew she wouldn't allow that.

The next morning, we told the kids Jaden would be living with grandpa.

Emma was very happy to have the bedroom all to her even though she said she would miss her sister.

I told the kids to keep Jaden in their prayers.

I got really worried when dad told me she came and took her things, but she wasn't staying at his house,

I didn't know where she was.

Ella and I were making cookies, when Aunt Tina called me to say Jaden showed up on her doorstep for me not to worry anymore.

I was so thankful. I prayed Aunt Tina and Paul would be able to help her.

Chapter thirty one

Coy and Ella had really bonded, she was the one that asked him, if she could call him dad, right after we moved back home I thought Coy was going to cry.

Even though now we had two more kids to care for we always made special time with each of them.

It had been six months and we still hadn't seen Jaden, Aunt Tina kept me informed about her.

She was working at a bank, and seemed to be getting her life in order, she didn't run around anymore.

I thanked God every day for my Aunt Tina.

One Sunday Morning Jaden came to church, I was so happy to see her.

"Hi Jaden" "Hi Aunt Sara, how are you?" "I'm fine, I have missed you"

She still seemed so distance.

Emma and Luke sat with her, Jaden mostly just kept her head down; I knew god was dealing with her heart.

As the weeks passed, more and more Jaden started coming around.

She helped me give Emma her eighteen birthday party, and she came to church every service.

It was on a Wednesday night that Jaden received the gift of the holy and was baptized...

We were so over joyed.

She had changed so much, but that is what happens when you turn to god.

He takes your heartache and turns it into joy.

She started acting her old self again before the tragedy of losing both of her parents happened.

She was loving and caring she stayed a big part of her sister and brother's lives.

Now I was glad to have her around Emma, because now she was a great influence.

I knew Sandra and Scott would be so proud of their children, I know I was.

Even though we were very proud of Emma leaving for college, it was also sad to see her go.

They were growing up so fast, just the other day Luke told us he liked a girl at church and planned on marring her when he turned eighteen. Coy and I told him we would talk more about it when he returned from college.

Chapter thirty two

Jaden wore a beautiful smile as she walked down the church aisle in her long wedding grown.

She had matured so much in these last few years, since she received the Holy Ghost; she was a joy to be around. A much respected young woman in our church

Her wedding colors were rose and everything was beautiful, she had seven Bride's maids that stood there waiting for her to finish her walk.

Then she took her spot next to the pastor's son.

What a beautiful couple they made.

Day by day I watched as God was healing her broken heart, so happy I served a prayer answering God, who loves us and cares about us, and see our brokenness.

There isn't a day that goes by that I don't think about my beautiful sister and I still miss her so much.

I remember one time she said to me. Sara if something was too happened to Scott and me, you wouldn't care for my children.

"Oh yes Sis because you have taught me that Children are a gift from god and we are very lucky that God trusted us with them."

As I look at Jaden, Emma Luke, and Ella I feel so blessed

These were now our children, and I wanted my sister to be at peace knowing they are loved.

We have taught them about god, we took them to church, and we showed them love.

When I look back on my life, I would have never guessed, I would be raising my sister's children.

All I ever wanted was this great career, traveling and seeing the world, wearing suits with high heels, being this important person.

When I stand back and look at my not so neat house and my mini van parked outside and socks and book bags on the floor.

All I can think is, I wouldn't trade this life for all the glamour in the world.

This was now my great career, and taking the kids to parks and ball games and church was seeing the real world.

And as far as wearing high heels I do that every church service, and I know now I'm a very important person I am a child of the King.

About the Author

Brenda is retired. She has four children, ten Grandchildren and four great grandchildren she lives in Michigan with her husband Duane, And their two mixed Maltese dogs. Calie & Zoey. This is the third book she has written in the series "The Damage of Deception"

Brenda and Duane are member of Grace Apostolic Tabernacle in South Haven, MI.

Book Four "A Promise Broken"

Dana had always wanted to be a school teacher, even as a little girl that was her dream.

When she was offered a fourth grade position five hours from her home and her mother, Dana took it.

She loved the excitement of her students. And it didn't take long for her to fall in love with every one of them.

But one night Dana would face a fear that would convince her to flee back to her home town.

Instead of running she put all of her trust in Jesus because she discovered that through God, she could face anything.

But out of that fear, came an amazing love.

And at the end she would learn that forgiveness comes with a great sacrifice.

Made in the USA
Lexington, KY
19 September 2019